D

A SURPRISE CONFRONTATION . . .

"We're the fellas you've been following all day," Clint said, "and we got tired of it. We thought we'd stop in and ask you why."

"Why what?" Bennett asked.

Haggerty made a move that surprised even Clint. He brought the butt of his pistol down on the point of Bennett's shoulder. The man cried out in pain and grabbed the wounded area.

"We're not stupid," Haggerty said, "so don't treat us like we are. Why are you following us?"

Bennett's eyes sought out Clint's. They were filled with pain, but they were also filled with fear.

"Whoever you're afraid of," Clint said, "they're not here and we are. Think about it."

DON'T MISS THESE
ALL-ACTION WESTERN SERIES
FROM THE BERKLEY PUBLISHING GROUP

THE GUNSMITH by J. R. Roberts

Clint Adams was a legend among lawmen, outlaws, and ladies. They called him . . . the Gunsmith.

LONGARM by Tabor Evans

The popular long-running series about U.S. Deputy Marshal Long—his life, his loves, his fight for justice.

SLOCUM by Jake Logan

Today's longest-running action Western. John Slocum rides a deadly trail of hot blood and cold steel.

J. R. ROBERTS

J

JOVE BOOKS, NEW YORK

THE FLYING MACHINE

A Jove Book / published by arrangement with
the author

PRINTING HISTORY
Jove edition / March 1997

The Putnam Berkley World Wide Web site address is
http://www.berkley.com/berkley

ISBN: 0-515-12032-4

A JOVE BOOK®
Jove Books are published by The Berkley Publishing Group,
200 Madison Avenue, New York, New York 10016.
JOVE and the "J" design are trademarks
belonging to Jove Publications, Inc.

PRINTED IN THE UNITED STATES OF AMERICA

10 9 8 7 6 5 4 3 2 1

THE
GUNSMITH
183
THE FLYING MACHINE

ONE

"How do you think birds fly?" Leena Gill asked.

Clint Adams was lying with his head in her lap, looking up at the sky. He had never thought much about *how* birds flew.

"I don't know."

Leena was playing with a lock of his hair as she also stared up at the sky.

"I've always wondered that, ever since I was a little girl," she said.

"How they fly?"

"How," she said, "why . . . and why we don't."

"That's easy," he said. "It's because we don't have any wings."

Next to them on the ground were the remnants of a picnic lunch. Leena lived in the town of Kellock, in Arkansas. Clint had been passing through on his way to nowhere in particular, and one look at her had been all the reason he'd needed to stay around for a while.

It took him two days of staying at the boardinghouse she owned and ran, eating meals cooked by her, helping her in the kitchen, stopping to talk to her whenever he had the chance. On the evening of the third day he ended up in her bed.

She was tall, with auburn hair, full breasts, a slender waist, long, graceful legs, and a wonderful butt. The thing that fascinated him the most, though, was her face. During sex she had the most expressive face he had ever seen on a woman. All of her feelings were reflected there, and whether he was kissing her breasts and biting her nipples, or running his tongue down over her belly, or rubbing his mouth over the smooth skin of her inner thighs, he knew exactly how she was feeling, because he saw it there. Also, she was vocal. She told him if she liked what he was doing or not, she cooed to him, caressed him with her hands, and he loved kissing that expressive mouth.

He was looking at her mouth now, only she kept lifting her chin to stare at the sky, at the birds that were flying overhead.

He remembered last night—their third together—and the way she looked while sitting astride him, riding him. Her eyes had been glazed, and as she rode up and down on him she gritted her teeth, or grimaced, but it was a sex grimace, sometimes accompanied by a grunt or a groan. He found her the most exciting woman he'd been with in a long time, and it was for this reason that he knew he had to leave soon.

But that was not something to be talked about now. Not after a wonderful picnic, and talk about birds.

"Let's stop talking about birds," he said, reaching up and putting his hand behind her neck.

He pulled her down to him so he could kiss her, and she laughed softly just before his mouth covered hers. She returned his kiss avidly, and slid his head from her lap so she could lie down beside him on the blanket.

The kiss progressed and soon they were undoing each other's clothes, peeling them off and discarding them. The afternoon sun felt good on their naked skin.

Clint began to concentrate on her breasts, which were large, round, and firm. The nipples hardened and stood out as he sucked and licked them. He slid one hand down over her belly and found her wet and slick. She stiffened as he touched her with his fingertips, just brushing her lightly for now, but it was enough to make her shudder and grab for him.

She closed her thighs on his hand, trapping him there, and reached down to cup his head as he kissed her belly. Soon she opened her thighs again, and he moved his hand and replaced it with his mouth. He lay flat on the blanket between her legs, slid his hands beneath her buttocks, lifted her off the ground, and began to lick her eagerly. She gasped and squirted onto his tongue, and he continued to suck and lick her until her belly began to tremble and she began to thrash about, calling out to him to never, ever stop, and at the same time trying to push him away because it felt too good. . . .

Later they switched positions so that Clint was lying on his back and Leena was bent over him. She took his rigid penis into her mouth and began to lick and suck him lovingly. She caressed his testicles with one hand while she held his penis at the base with the other. She rode him up and down with her mouth, wetting him thoroughly, bringing him to the brink of completion before releasing him and giving him a sly, lascivious look.

She got onto her hands and knees and presented him with a view of her splendid butt. He positioned himself behind her and reached between her thighs to touch her. As he stroked her she became wet again, and he was able to slide between her thighs and up into her easily. He began to move in and out of her, holding her by her hips. She started pushing back against him when he thrust himself into her so that they started making a slapping sound each time his belly struck her butt. The *slap-slap-slap* sound increased in tempo, faster and faster, until it was accompanied by her groans and his grunts. He felt something boiling up inside of him and even before he exploded into her he knew that this was going to be one of those times when the pleasure was going to be mixed with an exquisite kind of pain. . . .

TWO

Anyone watching the two riders wouldn't have known who was more tired, the two boys or the horses.

Wilbur Wright sat slumped on his horse, fighting to keep his eyes open.

Ahead of him rode his brother, Orville. The boys were fifteen and twelve, and neither was an accomplished rider. Having ridden from North Carolina to Arkansas had taken a lot out of them. Also, not knowing anything about horses, they had pushed their mounts right to the point of all endurance. As a result all four were weary and badly in need of some rest.

Wilbur, riding behind Orville, had no idea that his brother had fallen asleep in the saddle, so it came as a surprise to him when the younger Wright brother suddenly slipped from the saddle and fell to the ground. Of course, the resulting thud woke him.

"Wha' happened?" Orville demanded loudly, looking around.

"You fell asleep, that's what happened," Wilbur said, looking down at his brother.

"I did not," Orville said indignantly.

"Well, you fell off your horse."

Orville looked around and realized that he couldn't very well deny *that.*

"So I did," he said, "but I didn't fall asleep. I'm as awake as you are, Wilbur."

"That means you fell asleep."

Wilbur looked ahead of him and saw that Orville's horse had stopped at the top of a rise.

"Come on," he said, "let's get your horse."

He dismounted and helped his brother to his feet, then they walked together, leading Wilbur's horse.

"Wilbur?"

"What?"

"I'm hungry."

"So am I."

"Are we gonna starve to death?"

"We'll find something to eat."

"I'm starting to think this wasn't such a good idea."

"I told you if we had money we could have taken the train, but we didn't have any money. We had to take horses."

"No, I don't mean the horses," Orville said, "I mean the whole trip."

"Orville," Wilbur said, "we agreed on this trip."

"Well, you're the oldest," Orville said.

"What does that mean?"

"It means you should know better," Orville said. "I just went along with you."

"Orville . . ."

"What?"

"Never mind," Wilbur said, "just get your horse."

Orville went up the rise to get the animal, but when he reached it he suddenly began to wave to his brother. Wilbur looked around, found a large stone, put his horse's reins on the ground and the stone on top of them, and then went to join his brother.

"What is it—"

"Look."

Orville was pointing down the other side of the rise where a man and a woman were on a blanket, apparently having a picnic. Well, actually, they had already had their picnic. At the moment they were naked. The woman was on her hands and knees, and the man was on his knees behind her.

"What are they doing?" Orville asked.

"They're having sex, stupid," Wilbur said.

"Like that?" Orville asked. "From behind? They can do that?"

Wilbur was the older brother, and as such the more experienced. He had even been inside a whorehouse once.

"Of course they can," he said, although he wasn't at all sure how.

"Should we keep watching them?" Orville asked hopefully.

"Of course," Wilbur said, "we need a rest, don't we? Just make sure your horse doesn't run away."

"How?"

"Do what I did."

Orville was reluctant to leave the scene below them, but he walked his horse back to where his brother had left his and looked for a stone. He couldn't find one, so he used the same one. As a result the stone did not sit securely on both pairs of reins.

Orville hurried back up the rise.

"What are they doing now?" he asked.

"The same thing," Wilbur said, watching the two adults in fascination, "only faster!"

The boys continued to watch as the man and woman changed position and then continued to have sex.

"How can they do that for so long?" Orville asked.

"I don't know," Wilbur said.

"Aren't they worried about the sun burning them?"

"I don't know."

"What are they doing now?"

"I don't know!"

"Well, what do you know, Wilbur?"

Wilbur glared at his little brother and said, "I know that if you don't shut up I'm gonna knock you down this hill."

"You don't have to get sore," Orville said, and the boys continued to watch.

A few moments later Orville asked, "Won't *they* get sore?"

THREE

Hal Stockton reined his horse in then dismounted. Wendell Ward remained mounted and watched as his partner studied the ground.

"Well?" he asked, after a few moments.

"They came this way, all right," Stockton said. "I recognize the imprint."

Stockton had told Ward days ago that one of the horses the boys were riding had a distinct footprint. He had showed the print to Ward, who had not been able to see what was so special about it, but then he didn't have to. Stockton was the tracker.

Ward was the trigger.

Stockton stood up and brushed off his hands. Instead of mounting up again he stared up at Ward.

"What?" Ward asked.

"Do you think this is on the level?"

"Is what on the level?"

"You know, all this . . . flying stuff."

"I know two things, Stock," Ward said.

"What's that?"

"If man was meant to fly he'd have wings."

"And the other?"

Ward leaned forward in his saddle.

"When a man pays me to do a job, I don't ask questions."

Stockton knew that. Wendell Ward had said that to him many times before during their partnership.

Both men were roughly the same age, in their mid-thirties. They'd had limited success in their lives until they joined up with each other. Since then they had made a reputation for themselves as getting done any job they took on. With Stockton's ability to track, and Ward's abilities with a gun, they complemented each other perfectly. They each knew what their job was, and there was never any blurring of the lines.

"Come on," Ward said, "get mounted."

Stockton nodded and did so.

"How far ahead are they?" Ward asked.

"Still a day and a half, maybe two," Stockton said. "Why did they wait so long to hire us?"

"I don't know," Ward said, "I'm just glad they did. There's a lot of money in this for us, Stock, if we play our cards right."

"This ain't our usual kind of job, Wendell," Stockton said.

"I know it," Ward said, "that's why we're gettin' an unusual amount of money."

FOUR

After they had dressed they cleaned up the remnants of their picnic and loaded it all into the buggy they had rented. Clint now knew that they were being watched, but he didn't know for how long. He had heard two horses up on the rise.

"We're being watched," he said to Leena.

She looked alarmed, and embarrassed.

"How long have they been there?"

"Not long," he lied. "Only since we began clean up."

She looked relieved.

"Do you know who it is?"

"No," he said, "just that there are probably two of them."

Now she looked alarmed once again.

"Are they after you, Clint?" she asked. "For your reputation?"

"I don't know," he said. "It's possible. It's also possible they're just curious."

"Well," she said, "I'm glad they didn't come along sooner."

Clint remained silent.

"What will we do?"

"You drive the buggy back to town."

"What about you?" she asked.

"I'm going to see if I can ask our friends a few questions." He smiled to allay her fears. "I'll be back in town soon."

"Be careful."

"I always am."

As the woman climbed into the buggy, Wilbur and Orville stopped watching.

"She was pretty," Orville said as they turned their backs on the man and woman.

"Yes, she was."

"What do we do now, Wilbur?"

"We have to get moving."

"I'm still tired."

"If we're going to get to California, we have to keep moving," Wilbur said.

"I don't know why we have to go all the way to California."

"I told you," Wilbur said. "There's gold there, enough so that we can build our flying machine."

"Do you think it can really work?" Orville asked.

"It will work," Wilbur said, patting the saddlebag that held their plans, "and it will make us famous."

Orville remembered when his brother first started talking about men flying like birds. He had thought he was crazy, but the more Wilbur talked the more convinced

Orville became that it could be done. It would take money, though, and that's why they were traveling to California, where there was gold in the ground for the taking.

Or so the two boys thought.

Clint worked his way up the rise, wondering why it was so easy. If they were being watched by men who meant him harm, they'd probably still be watching. He was thinking that he'd been right when he told Leena that they may have been watching just out of curiosity.

Still, he wanted to know who was watching them.

He was working his way uphill, but was coming up the side. If they did look now, they wouldn't see him. He'd only been vulnerable to detection for a few minutes.

As he came to the top of the rise, he saw the two watchers lying on their backs, talking. He couldn't believe that it was two boys, one of whom looked to be in his teens. As he came up on them, they saw him and quickly got to their feet.

"So," Clint said, "my two Peeping Toms are boys, huh?"

"We didn't mean no harm!" the younger one said right away.

The older one puffed out his chest and said, "I'm not a boy."

"No," Clint said, "I guess you're a young man, but watching a man and a woman while they're . . . together, that's something a boy would do."

"I told you we shouldn't have watched," the younger one said.

"You did not," the older one said.

"Did, too."

"Did not."

"That's enough of that," Clint said, and both boys fell silent.

Clint looked them over and saw that they were badly in need of some rest. He looked down the other side of the rise and saw two horses moving about freely, getting further and further away by the minute. They, too, looked like they were in need of some rest.

"Looks like your horses are getting away."

"What?" the older one said. "Orville, what did you do?"

"I used the same rock—"

"It wasn't heavy enough!" Wilbur said.

"I didn't know, Wilbur!" Orville shouted back.

"You fellas better gather your horses up," Clint said, "and then we'll talk."

"What's there to talk about?" the older boy asked.

"Well," Clint said, "for one thing, how hungry you two must be."

"I'm real hungry, mister," the younger one said.

"Well, get your horses and we'll walk them into town. It's not far."

Orville ran down the hill toward the horses while Wilbur continued to study Clint.

"You must be hungry, too," Clint said.

Wilbur's stomach growled.

"Go on," Clint said, "go get your horse and we'll get something to eat."

"You ain't sore at us?"

"For what?"

"For watching you and, uh . . ."

"No," Clint said. "If I was your age, I would have watched, too. Is that your brother?"

"Uh-huh."

"Well, you better go and help him."

Wilbur looked at Clint a little longer, with some suspicion, and then went down the hill after his brother.

Clint didn't blame the boy for being suspicious. He was probably looking out for his brother more than himself. He wondered how far they had come, and how far they were going, and why they were traveling alone.

Those were all questions he would get the answers to later.

FIVE

The walk to town was only a couple of miles, but to the boys, in their condition, it seemed much longer. Clint didn't dare let them ride the horses, though. The animals looked like they were on their last legs and were about to drop.

When they reached town he decided to take the boys to Leena's boardinghouse and take care of them first, before the horses. The animals could at least take a rest while they were standing outside.

When he walked into the house, Leena came out into the foyer and gave him a curious look.

"What have we here?" she asked.

"Two tired and hungry boys," Clint said.

She gave him a questioning look, but he shook her off. In truth, he didn't have many answers himself.

"What would you like me to do with them?" she asked.

"How about feeding them while I take care of their horses?"

"And then?"

"And then I'll be back and we can all have a talk."

"Do you boys want to eat?"

Neither boy was able to look Leena in the face—not after the way they had seen her earlier.

"Yes'm," they both said, their cheeks coloring.

"Well, then, go into the kitchen and I'll be right there," she said. "You can wash your hands while you're waiting."

"Yes'm."

"Right through there," she said, pointing the way.

As they walked to the kitchen, Leena said to Clint, "Those boys are the ones who were watching us, aren't they?"

"Yes," Clint said, "and they're not dangerous."

"Maybe not," she said, "but did you see the color in their cheeks? I think they saw a lot more than you think."

Clint frowned and said, "I don't think so. I think they might have a fever."

"They look all worn-out," she said. "Maybe you should bring the doctor back with you to take a look at them."

"I might do that." He didn't know if she believed his fever remark, but having a doctor look at them might not be a bad idea.

"Were they traveling alone?"

"As far as I know," Clint said. "I haven't really asked them a lot of questions . . . yet."

"Well, then, I'll wait until you get back and you can ask the questions. I'll just get them fed and cleaned up."

"Okay."

He started for the door, but she spoke before he could reach it.

"And don't think for one minute I believe that line about a fever."

He hunched his shoulders and got out of there.

The boys were still eating by the time Clint returned with the town doctor. They looked cleaner—at least, their faces and hands did. Nothing would help their clothes.

"Are these the two lads we were talking about?" the doctor asked.

"This is them," Clint said.

"That's Orville," Leena said, "and that's Wilbur."

Obviously she had been talking to the boys while he was gone.

"Hello, boys."

The younger boy stared at the man with wide eyes, and then at the black bag he was carrying.

"Are you the doctor?"

"Yes, I am," the tall, slenderly built man said. "My name is Doctor Cross."

Orville looked at his brother, who was concentrating on the plate of cold fried chicken that was in front of him.

"There's nothing to be afraid of, Orville," Leena said, putting her hands on the younger boy's shoulders. "The doctor just wants to make sure you're okay."

"Yes'm."

"We can wait until the boys finish eating," Doctor Cross said.

"A cup of coffee, Andrew?"

Clint knew that Doctor Andrew Cross was in love with Leena. He didn't think they had ever been together, but figured the two of them probably would once he left town.

"Thank you, Leena."

Clint had walked the horses to the livery, where the liveryman had pronounced them to be crow bait. Clint asked the man to do the best he could by them. He then left there and went straight to the doctor's office. Cross had greeted him coldly but politely. The first time Leena had introduced Cross to Clint, the man had pegged him as a rival. In a way he was right, but only temporarily.

"Clint?"

"Yes, please," he said.

"Sit, both of you."

There were four chairs around the kitchen table and the men took the two remaining ones. Leena placed empty cups in front of them and then filled them.

"Well, it seems you've learned the boys' names."

"Yes," Leena said, "we've managed to get that far, but not much further."

"Where are you boys from?" Doctor Cross asked.

Orville looked at his older brother, who looked back only long enough to shake his head. Both boys then went back to eating.

"I guess they're not going to answer any questions," the doctor said. "Maybe we should take them over to the sheriff."

"What for?" Leena asked. "They're not criminals."

"No, but they are runaways," the doctor said. "Their parents are probably worried sick."

"Why don't you just examine them and make sure they're healthy, Doc?" Clint suggested. "We'll decide what to do with them after that."

Cross gave Clint an annoyed look. As a doctor he obviously thought he knew how to handle children. It was apparent to others, however, that he did not.

"All right," he said, standing up. He had not taken a sip of the coffee in front of him. "All right then, who's first?"

There was just a moment of hesitation and then Wilbur, the older boy, stood up and said, "I'll go first."

Cross looked at Leena.

"Do you have an empty room upstairs?"

"I have too many empty rooms, Andrew," she said. "Take the second door on the right. Number four."

"Fine," Cross said. "Wilbur, is it?"

"Yes, sir."

"Come along, then."

Cross led the way and Wilbur followed, trying to be brave for his brother.

Clint, still seated, took a drink from his cup and looked across the table at Orville.

"The doctor's kind of stuffy, isn't he?"

Orville looked at Clint and smiled in spite of himself.

"He's okay, though," Clint said. "He won't hurt you or your brother. Okay?"

"Okay."

"Do you want some more milk, Orville?" Leena asked.

"Please, ma'am."

While she poured him another glass, Clint said, "You and your brother must have come far."

Orville didn't answer.

"I mean, you're pretty tired, your horses are dragging their tails behind them. It just seems to me you must have come far, and quickly."

No answer.

Clint looked at Leena.

"I wonder where they're going in such an all-fired hurry?"

"Young boys are always in a hurry to get nowhere fast," she said. "I know, I had three brothers when I was growing up, and they were all in a hurry."

Clint didn't know if she was telling the truth or not. She had never before mentioned anything about brothers.

"Grown men, too," she added.

Clint studied Orville, who was now staring at the bottom of his glass. It was obvious he was not going to get anything out of the boy. He figured he might as well just wait until they had both been examined and had both rested up some.

"Could I have some more coffee, please?" he asked Leena.

SIX

The doctor came down with Orville following him. The boy went back to the table and sat next to his brother.

"Well, they're—" he started to say, but Clint quieted him and beckoned him to follow him from the room.

When they were in the foyer Clint said, "Okay."

"I was saying," Cross said, unhappy about having been interrupted, "they're healthy enough. A little malnourished, perhaps, but certainly nothing very serious—nothing a few good meals wouldn't cure."

"Well, that's good."

"Physically they're worn-out," Cross said. "They need some rest."

"They'll get it."

Cross looked appalled.

"You mean here? You're going to keep them here?"

"Why not?" Clint asked. "They're just children. They're no danger to anyone."

"What does Leena have to say about that?"

Perversely, Clint said, "Leena will go along with whatever I want to do."

Cross looked physically ill for a moment and then he said, "You'll have to excuse me. I have patients to see."

He brushed past Clint and went out the door. At that moment Leena came from the kitchen.

"Where's Andrew?"

"Oh, he's gone."

She put her hands on her hips.

"What did you do to him?"

"Nothing."

"What did you say to him?"

Clint spread his hands helplessly and said, "I just told him what we did on our picnic today."

"You—" she started, and then her eyes widened and she started to laugh. "I almost wish you had, just to see his reaction."

"I can catch him—"

"No! No, that's all right. What have you decided to do with the boys?"

"Well . . . you did say that you had a lot of empty rooms."

She didn't hesitate for a moment.

"Certainly they can rest here," she said, "but what do you intend to do with them afterward?"

"Well, if they continue to keep silent there's nothing I can do but send them on their way."

"Alone? Those two boys?"

"Wilbur is almost a man. He must be . . . fifteen."

"But look at them now. They've worn themselves to

a frazzle, and their horses, too. How long do you think they would last on their own?"

"I don't know," Clint said, "but what would you have me do, adopt them?"

She came closer to him so she could lower her voice.

"No," she said, "but you could find out where they want to go and then take them there."

"Why would I do that?"

"Well, along the way they might say something that would help you find out where they're from, and then you could telegraph their family."

"You want me to baby-sit!" he said.

"Hey," she said, "you're the one who found them. They're your responsibility."

"I can't—"

"Or we could turn them over to the sheriff, like Andrew said."

"We can't do that," he said. "The jail is no place for them."

"Well, if you don't help them you'll leave me no choice."

Clint shook his finger at her and said, "You're a wicked woman."

She gave him a saucy look and said, "We're not discussing that now, are we?"

That brought to mind a mental picture of her the way she had been in that meadow earlier, naked and with her behind to him . . . and he knew he was beaten.

SEVEN

When the boys were finished eating, they took them into the living room and sat them down on the sofa to talk to them.

"Now, I'm not going to pressure you boys to tell me where you came from," Clint said, "but if you want to talk to me, I'll listen."

The boys exchanged a glance, during which Clint felt that the older boy transmitted something to the younger. As brothers, they were obviously very close.

"Okay," Clint said, "will you accept our help for now?"

"What kind of help?" Wilbur asked.

"Well, more food, a place to sleep—I'm talking about a real bed."

Orville gave his brother a quick, pleading look.

"I'll bet you've been sleeping on the ground a lot."

"We have!" Orville said, and then fell silent when his brother gave him a quick look.

"Well," Leena said, "the beds are yours for the night, if you want them."

"You need the rest, boys," Clint said. "The doctor said you could get real sick if you don't rest."

"But we ain't sick now, are we?" Orville asked, concerned.

"No," Clint said, "you're not sick."

"That's good."

They may not have been sick, but now that they had eaten both boys were having trouble keeping their eyes open.

"I think it's time for you fellas to get some sleep," Leena said.

Orville's eyes popped open and he said, "It's still light out."

Every kid's argument, Clint thought. He had probably even said it himself a few times.

"Come on," Leena said, "I'll show you where your rooms are and see if I can find something for you to sleep in."

As the boys went up the stairs ahead of her, Clint sat on the sofa and thought the situation over. He'd been in Kellock for five days now, longer than he usually stayed in one place. It was probably time for him to be moving on. What harm would it do to take the two boys with him, at least for a while? Of course, those two "crow bait" specimens they were riding would not be able to keep up with Duke. He was going to have to get them two new horses and that was going to cost some money. He didn't mind helping the boys out, but if he spent money on them there was little chance that he'd ever get it back.

He was in the kitchen helping himself to another cup of coffee when Leena came down.

"They still can't look at me without blushing," she said.

"Well," Clint said, "maybe they saw a little more than I thought they did."

"Yeah, maybe."

"Are they asleep?"

"I'll bet they fell asleep as soon as their heads hit the pillows."

"Did you give them each their own room?"

"I tried to," she said, "but they wouldn't hear of it. They insisted on sleeping in one room, in one bed."

"I guess they're very close."

"I'd say."

She cleaned the remnants of the boys' impromptu meal from the table then turned to face him.

"What are you going to do about them?"

"I'll take them with me when I leave," he said. "I'll be traveling west anyway."

"When will you be leaving?"

"I want to give them enough time to rest," he said. "Probably day after tomorrow."

"That soon?" She looked sad.

He moved closer to her and put his hands on her shoulders.

"I probably would have been leaving then anyway, Leena," he said. "It's time for me to move on."

"I know," she said. "I guess I should be glad you stayed as long as you did. It's been a great few days, hasn't it?"

"It sure has."

She put her arms around him and they hugged.

"I knew you'd be leaving sooner or later," she said against his chest. "I just wish—"

"Wish what?"

She pushed away from him, her eyes misty, and said, "Oh, nothing. Get out of here now. I have to clean the kitchen and start dinner."

She cooked dinner for her boarders every night, the only meal that she supplied for them. The most boarders she could have at one time was twelve, and she now had only six, which was why she was able to offer each of the boys their own room.

"I'll be back for dinner," he said.

"Fine."

It was obvious that she wanted him to leave before she started crying.

"If the boys wake up before then, don't let them go out."

"You think they might run off?"

"Maybe."

"What would happen to them?"

"Who knows?" he said with a shrug. "They got this far alone, didn't they?"

"Yes," she said, "but this far from where?"

EIGHT

Clint left the boardinghouse and walked to the Kellock Saloon, one of the two saloons in town. The Kellock was small and did nothing more than serve drinks. The other saloon, called the Red Bull, offered gambling and entertainment. Kellock was a town that wanted to grow, and the Red Bull—a fairly new establishment—was its first step in that direction. There were factions in town that were warring over the opening of the Red Bull. Not everyone in town thought that a gambling parlor was a positive first step in growth.

Clint had been to both places and liked them both, but today he simply wanted a beer and a quiet place to think. The Kellock Saloon filled that bill.

He entered and strode up to the bar.

"Hello, Mr. Adams," the bartender greeted him.

"Jerry."

"What can I get for you?"

"A nice cold beer."

"Comin' up."

When the bartender returned with the beer, Clint said, "Thanks. I'll just take this to a table."

"Sure thing."

Clint went to a table in the back and sat down. He hadn't taken a sip of the beer when the batwing doors swung open and the sheriff of Kellock walked in. Instinctively, he knew the lawman was looking for him. Doctor Andrew Cross must have gone to the sheriff when he left the boardinghouse.

Clint drank from his beer mug and kept his eyes on the sheriff. The man looked around, spotted Clint in the back, and walked directly to his table.

Clint had spoken to the sheriff when he first arrived in town, just to let the man know he was there, and had not had much contact with him since.

Sheriff Stan Smith was a tall, sandy-haired man in his late thirties. Clint had thought him soft-spoken and mild when they'd met, and he recalled the man being somewhat nervous when he introduced himself by name.

"Afternoon, Mr. Adams," Sheriff Smith greeted.

"Sheriff."

"Mind if I sit for a spell?"

"Suit yourself," Clint said.

"I'll just get myself a beer."

"Fine."

"Will you have another?"

Clint raised his mug, which was still three quarters full, and said, "I'm still working on this one."

"Oh, right."

The man went to the bar, got himself a beer, and brought it back to the table. He sat across from Clint, with the beer in front of him, and seemed to promptly forget about it.

"Is there something I can do for you, Sheriff?" Clint asked.

"Well, actually," Smith said, "there is something I'd like to talk to you about."

"And what's that?"

"Well, I heard that you came into town in the company of two young strangers, two boys."

"That's right, I did."

"Well, I was wondering, uh, how they were."

"They're fine."

"Uh, how old are they?"

"I'm not sure," Clint said. "Twelve and fifteen, I guess."

The sheriff nodded, looked around, took a deep breath.

"Let me make this easy for you, Sheriff," Clint said. "What did Doctor Cross tell you?"

"Doctor Cross? Well, he . . . uh, he didn't—"

"Yes," Clint said, cutting him off, "he did."

The sheriff looked at him, then looked away.

"Well, he, uh, said that you and Miss Gill had two boys at her boardinghouse, and he thought they were runaways."

"And he thought that should concern you."

"Well, he said that the law should be concerned, but . . ."

"You didn't agree?"

"Well, I asked him what I could do, and he said he thought I should try to find out where they were from."

"Do you think this is your business, Sheriff?"

"Well, no . . . I mean, uh, well, the doctor thought . . ."

''Yeah, I know what the doctor thought,'' Clint said. ''Look, Sheriff, I don't know where the boys are from, but I'm going to find out. I'll be leaving Kellock with them, probably the day after tomorrow, and then there won't be any question about whether they're your concern or not.''

''Well, as long as you're going to look after them—''

''I am.''

''Well . . . I guess they're in good hands then.''

''I hope so.''

The sheriff nodded and stood up.

''Aren't you going to drink your beer?'' Clint asked.

''Well, actually, it's still a little early in the day for me.''

''I see.''

''Well, thanks for your, uh, help.''

''Sure.''

He nodded nervously, backed away a few steps, and then turned and walked out.

NINE

Clint nursed the rest of his beer and thought about Doctor Andrew Cross. Was he right? Should the boys have been turned over to the law as runaways? If every fifteen-year-old who ever ran away had been turned in as a runaway, the West probably never would have gotten settled. He himself had run away from the East and come west while still in his teens.

No, these boys deserved the same chance he had gotten. Several men had helped him in his youth, and here he had a chance to return the favor.

He finished the beer and left the saloon, waving to the bartender. He spent the rest of the afternoon getting everything ready for their departure the morning after the next.

• • •

Wendell Ward and Hal Stockton camped for the evening by a water hole that was roughly a day and a half's ride from the town of Kellock.

"These boys are either real smart or they're crazy," Stockton said. "They haven't stopped in a town for miles. How the hell are they eating?"

"There's another possibility," Ward said.

"What's that?"

"They're just plain dumb."

"Whatever the reason," Stockton said, "their horses should be half dead by now."

"They probably are," Ward said. "It's more than likely we'll find them afoot, or stuck in some town."

"Well," Stockton said morosely, "this is taking way longer than I expected it to."

"That's your problem," Ward said.

"What is?"

"You start a job expecting it to take just so long," Ward said. "You've got to be more flexible than that, Stock."

"Yeah, yeah."

Ward laughed then.

"What's so funny?"

"You're just upset that you haven't had a woman in a while."

"Yeah, well . . . I need to have a woman regularly, Wendell, you know that."

"I do know that, Stock," Ward said. "You need women like some men need food or water."

"Damn right."

Ward looked at his friend and partner and realized that he'd never known a more handsome man, or a man who had as much good fortune with women. As for Wendell

Ward, he'd never had much use for women—but then, as homely-looking as he was, they never had much use for him either.

"What's the next town?" Stockton asked.

Ward thought a moment.

"I think it's Ludlow, but beyond that is Kellock."

"What's so special about Kellock?"

"It's got a telegraph office."

"How do you know?"

Ward smiled.

"I remember."

Stockton could never understand how his friend could have such a good memory. He seemed to know everything there was to know about every decent-sized town in the West. He could hardly remember that last woman he had, and where it was.

"So it's got a telegraph office," he said. "So what? We got somebody to send a telegram to?"

"That makes it a decent-sized town, Stock," Ward said. "Maybe they stopped there for help."

"Well, I guess we'll just have to wait until we get there to see," Stockton said.

"I guess so."

"Hey," Stockton said, brightening, "if it's a decent-sized town it'll have whores, won't it?"

"Most likely."

"Maybe even a cathouse."

"Maybe."

Stockton was happier now, and bent to his task of making coffee to go with the beef jerky that would be their dinner.

TEN

Clint haggled with the liveryman for the boys' two pieces of crow bait, but it wasn't easy.

"Whataya expect me to give ya for them?" the man demanded.

"They're not so bad," Clint said.

"They're half dead."

"Well, all they need is to be fed, and to have some care taken with them," Clint said. "The right kind of man with the right touch could make fine animals out of them."

"Jesus," the liveryman said, "if ya wanna fuck me that bad why don't you kiss me first?"

They dickered some more and, in spite of himself, the liveryman was flattered by Clint's faith in him. He gave Clint a reasonable break on two nice enough animals.

"If you don't ride 'em into the ground they'll last ya awhile," he said.

"Don't worry," Clint said, "nobody's going to ride them into the ground."

After the livery he went to the general store to make arrangements for supplies. He'd need to carry a little more than he usually did when he was traveling alone . . . but a little more of what? He wasn't used to traveling with two boys. What should he buy for them? Did they drink coffee? Eat beef jerky? Well, anyone could eat beef jerky.

He left the store with jerky, coffee, some canned peaches, some bacon, and some beans. He also bought two new canteens, so each boy could have his own water. They had been sharing a canteen that had seen better days. Unfortunately, he couldn't afford to buy them new saddles, so they were going to have to keep the ones they had. He made arrangements to pick up the supplies the next day. There was no sense in taking them with him almost forty-eight hours ahead of time.

When he returned to the boardinghouse, Leena was setting the table for dinner.

"Did they wake up?" he asked.

"Not yet," she said, "or if they did, they haven't come down."

"They didn't slip out a window, did they?"

She turned to him and put her hands on her hips.

"I looked in on them twice, and they were still there. Besides, even if they are inexperienced travelers, they'd know that they couldn't get very far on foot, wouldn't they?"

"One would hope so," he said.

"Are you going to have dinner with the others?" she asked.

He took a deep breath, appreciating the delicious smells that were coming from the kitchen.

"I wouldn't miss another of your meals, Leena," he said.

From the glum look that came over her face, it was clear that she took that as a reminder that he'd be leaving soon.

"I'll get cleaned up for dinner."

"It won't be for twenty minutes yet," she said. "You might want to look in on those boys."

"All right."

They both left the dining room, she to go to the kitchen and he to go upstairs.

He went into his own room first and washed up, using the water basin and pitcher on the dresser. After that he walked down to the room the boys were sleeping in and opened the door. As he peered in, Wilbur, the older boy, looked at him from the bed and held his finger to his lips to indicate that Orville was still asleep.

Clint beckoned Wilbur to come to him, which the boy did, quitting the bed without waking his brother. Clint drew him out into the hall.

"I don't want Orville to wake up and find me gone," Wilbur said.

"I won't keep you long. Dinner is in about twenty minutes. If he wakes up, just come on down. We'll set two places for you."

"All right," Wilbur said, touching his stomach. "I am kind of hungry again."

"Then after dinner we have to talk."

"About what?"

"About where you and your brother are going, and if I'm going the same way."

"Which way are you going?" Wilbur asked.

"West."

"That's where we're going."

"Not on those horses you rode in on," Clint said.

"We can't afford no others."

"Well," Clint said, "if you ride with me for a while I might be able to arrange for fresh horses."

"Really?" Wilbur asked excitedly, but then quickly regained control of himself. "Why would you do that?"

"I want to help you."

"But why?"

"Because you need it," Clint said. "What other reason would there be?"

"Ain't nobody wanted to help us up to now."

"Well, I do. Maybe I can even get you where you're going . . . wherever that is."

Wilbur did not respond.

"All right," Clint said, "go back inside before your brother wakes up. I'll see you down at dinner."

Wilbur nodded and went back into the room.

It was clear he was going to have to gain the boys' trust before they would tell him everything. It was also clear that might not be an easy task.

ELEVEN

Including Clint there were five of Leena's boarders at the table for dinner. He was the fifth diner.

"Who are the other two places for?" Cardwell, the drummer, asked. He was a weasely-looking man with thinning hair combed across a balding pate, and had an annoying way of wrinkling his nose when he talked. That's what made Clint think of a weasel when he looked at the man.

"We have two new guests in the house," Leena said. "Two boys."

"How young?" Travers asked. Dalton Travers was in his fifties and couldn't stand kids, especially small ones. He was doing some business in town that Clint didn't know about, but he did know that the man had chosen Leena's to stay at only after he made sure there were no children living there.

"They're young boys, twelve and fifteen, Mr. Travers," Leena said, "and they won't bother anyone."

"How long they staying?" Travers asked peevishly.

"Just until day after tomorrow," Clint said. "They'll be leaving, and so will I."

"Time to move on, eh, Mr. Adams?" Silas Harper asked. Harper was in his thirties, a mild-mannered man who was some kind of surveyor for the government.

"That's right, Mr. Harper."

"Should get yourself a steady job, Mr. Adams, like I got," Harper said. "I get paid regular, and I still get to travel."

"Long as you kiss the right ass in Washington, eh, Harper?" Travers asked, laughing.

"I don't do that, Mr. Travers," Harper said, "and I'll thank you not to say that I do."

"Ah," Travers said, and continued to shovel in Leena's meat loaf without a word of how good it was. Everyone else had commented on it except him.

The final diner at the table was Ben Haggerty. Clint didn't know what Haggerty did for a living either, but the man was quiet, never complained, and was always polite to Leena. He was in his thirties, a big fellow, tall and powerfully built. He was ignoring the conversation going on around him and was giving all of his attention to the meal. Clint had the feeling Haggerty was a man of action, and probably good at what he did. The good ones could afford to be quiet and polite. They had nothing to prove to anyone. What he didn't know was whether Haggerty was a lawman, a bounty hunter, an outlaw, or something else entirely—like himself.

They were about fifteen minutes into the meal when

Wilbur and Orville Wright appeared from upstairs, entering the dining room tentatively.

''Here are our young guests now,'' Leena said, standing up and walking over to them. She put her hand on each of their shoulders in turn as she introduced them. ''This is Wilbur, and this is his brother Orville. I, uh, don't know their last name.''

''Wright,'' Orville said before he could stop himself. That drew him a hard look from his brother. Wilbur hunched his shoulders and looked away.

''Come on, boys. I have your places set.''

The boys sat on a side of the table across from Travers—who scowled at them—and Harper. They were seated between Leena and Clint.

She got them to their seats, poured them some milk, and told them to help themselves.

''Thank you, ma'am,'' Orville said. ''I'm very hungry.''

''Well, you eat all you can, Orville. There's more where that came from.''

Both Wilbur and Orville stocked up on meat, vegetables, biscuits, and gravy. There didn't seem to be anything on the table—not the greens, not the carrots—that they didn't like.

''So where are you boys from?'' Harper asked.

Orville deliberately filled his mouth with food at that moment, leaving his older brother to answer the questions.

''East,'' Wilbur said.

''How far east?'' Harper asked.

''Pretty far.''

Harper leaned forward and asked, ''Don't you know the name of the place you're from, boy?''

Wilbur stared back at Harper with steady eyes and said, "I know."

Harper sat back and said, "The lad's got sand. See the way he stared back at me?"

"Leave him alone."

Everyone looked down at the table at the man who spoke, and they all looked surprised.

It was Haggerty.

"What?" Harper asked, not sure he'd heard right.

"You heard me, Harper," Haggerty said in a deep voice. "Leave the boy alone and let him eat. Don't be interrogatin' him."

Clint detected a hint of a southern accent in Ben Haggerty.

"I think Mr. Haggerty is right," Clint said. "These boys just want to eat, like the rest of us. Why don't we let them?"

"Runaways," Travers said.

"What?" Harper asked.

"If they don't want to talk," Travers said, "they must be runaways."

"We're travelers," Wilbur said, "that's all."

"Traveling to where?" Harper asked.

Wilbur looked the man in the eye and said, "West."

"Well," Harper said, "I guess that's about all we're gonna get out of this young fella, huh?"

"Don't pay them no mind, boy," Haggerty said. "You don't want to talk, you don't have to."

Wilbur looked at Haggerty and appeared impressed with the man's physical size. Clint's best guess was that the man was at least six and a half feet tall, with the broadest shoulders he'd ever seen. Every so often he'd catch Leena looking Haggerty over, too. Maybe when he was gone, it wouldn't be Doc Cross who would replace him in her affections.

"Thank you, sir."

Nobody questioned the Wright brothers for the remainder of the meal.

TWELVE

After dinner Clint decided he should probably talk to Wilbur without Orville, so he had Leena take the younger boy into the kitchen with her to help with the dishes. When he complained that it was women's work, Clint was surprised to find Haggerty volunteering to help, as well. Orville's eyes went wide at the prospect of a man the size of Ben Haggerty doing dishes, and he went into the kitchen without any further argument.

Clint took Wilbur outside for a walk, and a talk.

"Wilbur, I'd like to try and get you to trust me."

"How?"

"Well, for one thing, if you don't want to go back to where you came from, I'm not going to try to force you."

"Why not?"

"Because I left home when I was about your age," Clint said.

"Where was that?"

Hiding a grin, Clint said, "Back East." Wilbur did not question him further.

"And have you been out west all this time?" Wilbur asked.

"Yes."

They walked along in silence for a few moments, and then Wilbur asked, "Have you ever been to California?"

"Yes."

A pause, and then, "San Francisco?"

"Yes, I've been to San Francisco."

They walked in silence.

"Is that where you're headed?" Clint asked. "San Francisco?"

Wilbur didn't answer.

"Because if you are," Clint went on, "I have some friends there. I can give you their names and you can look them up when you get there."

No reply.

"In fact, I can send them a telegraph message to expect you. You'd have a place to stay."

"We're not headed for San Francisco . . . exactly."

Now it was Clint's turn to remain silent. He decided to let Wilbur tell it in his own time.

"We are headed for California, though."

"Uh-huh."

"But I can't tell you why."

"Do you want my help?"

"Would you help without knowing why we're going?"

"Sure," Clint said, "why not? I just want to get you where you're going safely."

"Then yes," Wilbur said, "we'd like your help."

"Good. And will you trust me?"

"I don't know," Wilbur said. "Maybe . . . how do you mean?"

"I mean will you do what I tell you to do."

"Grown-ups are always trying to tell kids what to do."

"You're not so much a kid anymore, are you, Wilbur?" Clint asked.

"No."

"Then isn't it time you stopped thinking of people older than you as grown-ups?"

Wilbur shrugged and said, "I guess."

"That's a boy's answer, Wilbur."

"All right then, yes, it is time."

"I'm only asking if you'll do what I tell you because I'm experienced at riding the trail, and you're not. You almost killed yourselves, and your horses."

"Are our horses all right?"

"No," Clint said, "I'll get you some new horses."

"We—we don't have much money."

"I'll trade your horses," Clint said. "You won't need to spend any money."

"What about you?"

"What about me?"

"We can't pay you."

"I didn't ask to be paid, Wilbur," Clint said. "I just said I wanted to help you. Is that okay?"

Wilbur started to shrug, then stopped himself.

"Sure," he said, "it's okay."

"Do you want to talk to Orville about this?"

"I'll talk to him," Wilbur said, "but he'll do what I tell him."

"Because you're older?"

"That's right."

"Well, then, is the day after tomorrow too soon for us to leave?" Clint asked.

"No," Wilbur said, "day after tomorrow is fine, but . . ."

"But what?"

"Well . . . what about Miss Leena?"

"What about her?"

"Well . . . are you two gettin' married, or something?" Wilbur asked.

"No."

"You ain't?"

"No, we're not."

"But I thought . . ."

"You thought what?"

Wilbur's face colored and he said, "Nothing. Were you, uh, gonna leave town anyway?"

"Yes, I was."

"I thought you lived here."

"No," Clint said, "I don't really live anywhere. I just travel a lot."

"Sounds great."

"Sometimes it is, Wilbur," Clint said, "and sometimes it isn't. Come on, let's go back to the house."

THIRTEEN

Wilbur talked with his brother Orville in their room later that night. He explained about Clint wanting to help them get to California.

"What do you think?"

"I like Mr. Haggerty," Orville said.

"What?"

"I like Mr. Haggerty," Orville said again. "I think we should ask him to help us."

"We didn't ask Mr. Adams," Wilbur pointed out, "he offered to help us. If we ask Mr. Haggerty for help we'll have to pay him."

"He's a nice man," Orville said. "Maybe he won't want to be paid."

"Everybody wants to be paid, Orville."

"Then why doesn't Mr. Adams?"

"He says he's leaving town anyway, riding west, and we can go along with him."

"When?"

"Day after tomorrow."

"Will our horses be ready by tomorrow, Wilbur?"

"Mr. Adams said he'll take care of that for us."

"How?"

"He's going to get us two new horses."

Orville looked even more puzzled.

"How? We don't have any money."

"He's going to trade our horses in."

Orville thought this over for a few minutes, his twelve-year-old face set very seriously, and then said, "I still think we should ask Mr. Haggerty."

"Why?"

"He's bigger."

"Never mind," Wilbur said, "just get ready for bed."

Clint and Leena were in bed together in her room, after having made love rather strenuously.

"I know what it is," he said. "You're trying to kill me so you can keep my body here."

"I'm just trying to give you something to remember me by."

"Oh, well, you've done that already."

"I just want to make sure."

They lay silently for a few moments and then Clint asked, "So, was Mr. Haggerty very helpful in the kitchen?"

"Not very," she said, "but he was wonderful with Orville. That little boy's eyes just shine now when he looks up at Ben."

"Ben?" he said. "It's Ben now?"

"Yes," she said, "and he calls me Leena."

"I see," Clint said. "Setting up my replacement already, huh?"

"Maybe."

"I thought it would be the young doctor."

"Andrew Cross?"

"He's in love with you."

"Oh, I know that."

"How do you feel about him?"

"He's a friend."

"Nothing more?"

"Of course not."

They were quiet for a time, and just when he thought she may have fallen asleep she said, "He doesn't like you, though . . . at all."

"Well, the feeling is mutual."

"Why?"

"He's a little . . . stuffy."

"Stiff-necked."

"Right . . . superior."

"Yes. . . ."

She moved around a bit, getting more comfortably pressed up against him.

"What happened with Wilbur?"

"He's generously agreed to let me help them."

"Where do they want to go?"

"California."

"For what?"

"Who knows?"

"He won't tell you?"

"No," Clint said, "he doesn't trust me that much yet."

"Why do you think they want to go there? Do they have family in California?"

"He didn't say, but I don't think that's the case."

"Then what?"

"I don't know, Leena," Clint said. "Maybe they've

read so much about it they just want to go and see it."

"What about their family back East?"

"He didn't say a word about them."

"Do they have any?"

Clint shrugged.

"What will you do, then?" she asked. "Take them all the way to California?"

"No," Clint said, "I haven't been planning a trip to California, and I'm not about to go now."

"Well, then, I don't understand. How far will you go with them?"

"I don't know," Clint said. "I haven't thought or planned that far. I thought I'd get them to trust me and start talking to me, and then maybe I could find out where they were from."

"And take them back there?"

He hesitated, then said, "No."

"Why not?"

"Because if I force them to go back they'll probably just run away again."

"Then you do think they're runaways."

"They're traveling cross-country without their parents, or any guardian, so yes, my guess is that they ran away."

"And you don't think you should force them to go back?"

"No," Clint said. "They're going to have to decide that on their own. I'm just going to have to help them make their decision."

"They don't know who you are, do they?"

"Not everyone knows who I am, Leena."

"Do you want to tell them?"

"No," he said. "I'd rather just be some man who's helping them along the way."

"A nice man," she said, sliding her hand over his belly. "You've helped me, you know."

"In what way?"

She giggled and said, "Lots of ways, but mostly you've restored my faith in men."

"How so?"

"You've shown me there are still some good ones out there."

"There are a lot of good ones, Leena," he said. "You just have to find them and then try them on for size."

"I hope I find one your size," she said, sliding her thigh over his and then straddling him. He was hard and he slid right into her. She closed her eyes, groaned, and said, "You fit me just right."

FOURTEEN

Clint spent much of the next day getting ready to leave. He spent the morning exercising Duke and making sure he was fit to travel. He also gave a good look to the two horses he'd "traded" with the liveryman for. They'd never keep up with Duke, but then Clint didn't intend to push them. For the Wright brothers, they'd do fine.

In the afternoon he sent a telegram to his friend Rick Hartman, in Labyrinth, Texas. Rick was expecting him shortly, and he had to let him know that he would be a little longer in showing up than he had originally thought. From the telegraph office he picked up the supplies from the general store, took them to the boardinghouse, and stored them in Leena's cellar.

"How have the boys been?" Clint asked. It sounded strange coming out of his mouth. It was also a very domestic-looking scene, with Leena in the kitchen and him asking about "the boys."

He had to admit to himself that he didn't like it. He had never thought that marriage and kids were in his future, so he had never considered it. Now he knew he was right. This just didn't feel like him. Suddenly, he was anxious to be on his way.

"They've been quiet, staying in their room," Leena said, and then added, "except for breakfast and lunch."

"Have they said anything?"

"Wilbur won't talk to me," she said, "but Orville did after lunch."

"Oh? What about?"

"Oh, this and that."

"Well, start with the this," Clint suggested, "and then go on to the that."

"He mostly talked about Ben Haggerty. He wanted to know if I thought Ben would help them for free."

"What did you say?"

"I said they'd have to ask Ben. I also said that I understood that you were going to help them."

"And what did he say?"

"He sort of shrugged and said . . . now remember, he's a little boy."

"I can take it."

"He said Ben was younger and bigger."

"Well," Clint said, "he's right about that."

"I talked to him a little," she said.

"This and that?"

"Yes. I don't think you'll have any problems with him when you start traveling."

"I don't anticipate any," Clint said. "Wilbur's the older brother. Orville will do what he says."

"Andrew was also here today."

"Cross, the sawbones? What did he want . . . as if I didn't know."

"Stop it," she said. "He checked the boys again and then inquired about them to me. I told him I didn't know any more than I did yesterday, when they arrived. He said he went to the sheriff."

"He did," Clint said, "and the sheriff came to me."

"You didn't tell me that."

"I guess I didn't think it was important."

"What did you tell him?"

Clint recounted his conversation with the sheriff.

"You were right," she said when he was done.

"About what?"

"It wasn't important."

"Thanks."

"What are you going to do the rest of the day? Do you want some lunch?"

"I'll wait until dinner."

"You'll be here for dinner?"

"My last chance to have your cooking?" he asked. "You can bet I'll be here."

"I can get up in the morning and make you breakfast before you leave," she offered.

"I don't think you'll be able to."

"Why not?"

He grinned and said, "You'll be too tired. See, I intend to give you something to remember me by tonight."

FIFTEEN

Ward and Stockton stayed in Ludlow only long enough to get a beer and a meal, and then they were on their way again.

"How long before we get to Kellock?" Stockton asked. They had stopped to have coffee and jerky for lunch, and to rest the horses.

"We could push it and make it by tonight, maybe," Ward said. "Or we could camp tonight and get there in the morning."

"What do you want to do?"

"Why don't we just wait and see where we are when it starts to get dark."

"This is startin' to get ridiculous," Stockton said.

"What is?"

"Trailin' two little kids across the country. Why don't people keep their kids home where they belong?"

"It's not the kids' parents who hired us, if you remember."

"I remember. What is it that's so all-fired special about these kids anyway?"

"I don't know, Stock."

"Didn't you ask?"

"No."

"Ain't you curious?"

"Nope."

"Why not?"

"We been ridin' together long enough for you to know I ain't the curious type, Stock," Ward explained. "It just ain't in me to ask questions when I don't need to know the answers to do my job."

"Well, I ain't like that," Stockton said. "I'm damned curious about these boys."

Ward dumped the remnants of his coffee into the campfire and stood up.

"Well, I tell you what, pard," he said. "When we catch up to them, you can ask them."

"I might just do that," Stockton said. "Yessir, I just might."

They broke camp and mounted up. They had not bothered to unsaddle their horses since they hadn't intended to be camped for long.

"I'm curious about somethin' else, too, Ward." He never called his partner Wendell. Ward hated his first name. The first time he told Stockton that, the other man had asked why he didn't have a nickname. Ward said he did. It was "Ward."

"Now what?"

"Well, why did you take this job in the first place?" Stockton asked.

"I already told you," Ward said, "it was for the money."

"You ain't told me how much we're gettin'."

Ward grinned and said, "I didn't want to make you nervous, Stock."

"That much?" Stockton asked with wide eyes.

"That much."

"Who are we workin' for?"

"That's something you don't have to know, Stock," Ward said. "I take care of the business end, remember?"

"Yeah, I remember," Stockton said. "I'm just curious, is all."

SIXTEEN

The next morning Clint rose without waking Leena, although he did intend to wake her to say good-bye. He went back to his own room for his saddlebags, and then went to the boys' room to wake them up. He was surprised to find them up, dressed and sitting on the bed, waiting.

"How long have you boys been up?" he asked.

"Since first light," Wilbur said.

"That's when I thought I got up."

"Real first light," Orville said. "When it was just a little patch in the sky."

"Oh."

"Are you ready to go?" Wilbur asked.

"I'm ready," Clint said. "You boys ready?"

"We're ready," Wilbur said.

Both boys stood up from the bed.

"Can we say good-bye to Miss Leena?" Wilbur asked.

"Sure," Clint said. "We'll wake her up."

"And Ben?" Orville asked.

"Uh, no, Orville," Clint said, "I don't think I'll wake Ben Haggerty up."

"You talked to him last night," Wilbur told his brother.

"So? You talked to Miss Leena yesterday."

"Hush up now, Orville," Wilbur said. "We're saying good-bye to Miss Leena and leaving."

"But—"

"I don't want to hear no more about it!" Wilbur scolded him. He looked at Clint. "We're ready."

"Let's go then."

They woke Leena and she came downstairs with them to see them off.

At the door she hugged each of the boys, which made them blush. In particular Orville, especially when she was holding him to her and he remembered the way he had first seen her. He could feel the curves of her body beneath her nightgown, and he was embarrassed because his body reacted like a man's.

Lastly she hugged Clint tightly.

"If you come back this way you better stop in and see me," she said urgently.

"I will, but you'll probably have a husband by then."

She smiled at him and said, "He'll just have to understand. We're friends."

He handed her a piece of paper with Rick Hartman's address in Labyrinth, Texas.

"If you ever need me for anything, this man will know where to find me."

She closed the slip of paper inside her hands and kissed him gently.

"You be careful," she said. "Don't let anything happen to these boys."

"They'll be fine."

She looked at the young Wright brothers and said, "You boys mind what Clint says, okay? He'll make sure you get where you want to go."

"Yes, ma'am," they said in unison.

"Come on, fellas," Clint said. "We better get going."

They each took a share of the supplies to carry and the three of them started walking to the livery.

At the livery Clint watched as Orville and Wilbur inspected their new horses.

"I don't know much about horses, Clint," Wilbur said, "but these sure look like fine ones."

"They're a little better than what you had," he said, saddling Duke. "You need some help saddling them?"

"We can do it," Wilbur said.

As it turned out, Wilbur, taller than Orville, had to help his younger brother get the saddle up on his horse, and then they cinched it in together.

When the horses were saddled they walked them outside. Clint was surprised to find Ben Haggerty standing there.

"Ben!"

Orville ran to Haggerty, who lifted the boy off the ground. It was then that Clint realized that the two had somehow forged some sort of bond. He wondered if he would ever get both boys to trust him the way Orville already seemed to trust Ben Haggerty.

The big man put Orville down, walked him to his

horse, and helped him into the saddle. He then turned to face Clint.

"You take care of these boys, Adams."

"You're welcome to come along, Ben."

"I would," Haggerty said, "but I've got other things to do."

Haggerty put his hand on Orville's arm, tapped Wilbur on his knee, and then turned and walked back toward the boardinghouse. Clint wondered idly if anything would develop between the big man and Leena.

"Are you happy?" Wilbur asked Orville. "You got to say good-bye to Ben."

"I'm happy," Orville said.

Clint mounted up.

"You boys ready to ride?"

They both nodded and Wilbur said, "We're ready, Clint."

"Then let's go."

SEVENTEEN

Four hours after Clint rode out of Kellock with the Wright brothers, Wendell Ward and Hal Stockton rode in.

Ward and Stockton left their horses at the livery and went to the nearest hotel to get rooms. After that they went to the nearest saloon.

"No women," Stockton complained as they walked in.

"It's early, Stock," Ward said. "Those women work late and sleep late. They'll be out and about later on. Let's just be thankful this place is open at noon and we can cut the trail dust with a beer."

They went to the bar and Ward ordered two cold beers.

"Only kind we got," the bartender said cheerfully.

"Maybe you can help us out," Ward said to the man.

He meant to take advantage of the man's apparent good nature.

"Sure, if I can."

"We're lookin' for someone."

"Just ride in, did ya?"

"That's right," Ward said. "We just rode in and we're lookin' for someone."

"Who might that be?"

"Two boys travelin' alone," Ward said.

The man hesitated, then asked, "You kin?"

Ward hesitated this time, then indicated Stockton and said, "He is. They're his nephews. They ran away from home and we're lookin' for them to take them back."

"Runaways, huh?"

"That's right," Stockton said, playing along.

"I figured that."

"You did?"

"Sure did."

"How come?"

The bartender shrugged.

"Two boys travelin' alone like that, with no parents, no adults, it figured."

"So you saw them?" Ward asked.

"Actually, no, I didn't . . . but I heard tell of them. Whole town did, really."

"Is that a fact?" Ward asked. "Why would that be?"

"The doctor."

Ward waited a few moments, then asked, "What about the doctor?"

"He talked about them. See, he thought they should be turned over to the sheriff."

"Were they hurt? Is that why the doctor saw them?"

"He just looked 'em over," the bartender said. "Far as I know, they wasn't hurt."

"Well, that's good," Ward said. "Ain't that good, Stock?"

"Huh? Oh, that's real good," Stockton said. "Say, bartender, when do the ladies come to work?"

"Ladies? Oh, we got no women workin' here. For that you'll have to go to—"

"We can find out about that later," Ward said, cutting the bartender off. "Right now maybe you can tell us where to find that doctor . . . what was his name?"

"Doctor Cross," the bartender said. "Sure, he's just down the street a ways. You can't miss 'im. . . ."

Ward and Stockton finished their beers and left the saloon.

"What a place," Stockton said in disgust. "No women. Why didn't you let him tell me where the women were, Ward?"

"We'll find the women later, Stock," Ward said. "Right now I want to talk to that doctor."

"Why are you worried about them boys' health?"

"The doctor can tell us where they are, Stock. Healthy or not we'll have them."

"Oh, yeah. . . ."

"Come on," Ward said, "the bartender said it was this way. . . ."

When the two men walked into Andrew Cross's office, he studied both of them. He could usually pick out the sick or injured party whenever someone came to see him, but these two men looked healthy—tired, but healthy.

"Can I help you gentlemen?" he asked.

"Yeah," Ward said, "we're lookin' for someone and we understand you know where they are."

"Oh? And who is this someone?"

"It's two people, actually," Ward said. "Two boys, traveling alone."

"Are you related to these boys?"

"My friend is," Ward said, indicating a bored-looking Stockton.

"They're my nephews," Stockton said, taking his cue. "My brother's boys. Him and his wife are real worried about them."

"Are they runaways?"

"They sure are," Stockton said. "They're givin' us a hell of a chase."

"I heard you examined the boys," Ward said.

"That's right."

"Were they okay?"

"Nothing a few meals and some sleep wouldn't cure."

"That's good. Can you tell us where they are?"

"I can tell you where they were," Cross said.

"How's that?"

"They were staying at a boardinghouse here in town."

"They *were* staying?" Ward asked.

"That's right," Cross said. "They left this morning."

"Alone?"

"Well, as a matter of fact, no, they did not leave alone. They left with a man."

"Who was the man?"

"A very impertinent man," Cross said, "who, if he had taken my advice and turned those boys over to the sheriff, might have saved you gentlemen—"

"Who was the man?" Ward asked again, forcefully.

Cross seemed surprised by the man's vehemence.

"His name is Adams, Clint Adams."

"Adams?" Stockton asked. "You mean—"

Ward nudged Stockton into silence.

"Do you know where they went, Doctor?"

"Well, no, I don't," Cross said. "I didn't see them leave."

"This Adams, he didn't tell you where he was taking the boys?"

"We were not exactly on friendly terms."

"Is there anyone in town who Adams *was* on friendly terms with?"

Cross opened his mouth to reply, then thought better of it and closed his mouth, hesitating before finally answering.

"Well, no, not really."

Ward and Stockton exchanged a glance. They knew when someone was lying to them.

"Doctor," Ward said, as he and Stockton moved closer to the man, "I'm gonna ask you that question once again. . . ."

EIGHTEEN

When Leena Gill opened her door in answer to a knock, she was surprised to find Andrew Cross standing on her doorstep with two strange men. She was also surprised to see that Cross was cut in the right-hand corner of his lower lip, as if he'd been struck a blow.

"Andrew, what—"

"Sorry to bother you, ma'am," Ward said, "but we were wondering if you could help us."

"Help you . . . with what? Andrew, what's going on? What happened to your—"

"They're looking for Adams, Leena," Cross said, cutting her off. "Just tell them where he went and they won't hurt us."

"Wha—"

"The doctor's right, ma'am," Ward said, "just tell us what we want to know and nobody gets hurt."

Leena was very uncomfortable under the other man's

gaze. Stockton, anxious for a woman, was looking Leena over hungrily.

"I'm going for the sheriff," Leena said, making as if to leave the house.

Stockton blocked her path.

"Can't let you leave, ma'am."

"I don't understand—"

"You don't have to understand," Ward said. "Just answer the question."

"Don't say anything, Leena."

The voice came from behind the men. As they turned, Leena saw that Ben Haggerty was standing in front of the house. His feet were spread about eighteen inches apart, his weight evenly distributed. His large right hand was hanging down by his gun.

"This ain't none of your affair, friend," Stockton said.

"Maybe not," Haggerty said, "but I'm making it mine. Now you," he said, indicating Ward, "let the doctor go, and you," pointing to Stockton, "move away from the lady."

"Maybe you can help us," Ward said, releasing his hold on Cross, "and avoid any trouble."

"Help you how?"

"We're looking for someone," Ward said. "Clint Adams, and two boys. We just want to know where they were going when they left town."

"I don't know where they were going," Haggerty said, "but I know what direction they were going."

"Well," Ward said, "that sure would help a lot."

"Ben, don't . . ." Leena said.

Haggerty raised his left hand to her and said, "Quiet, Leena. Let me handle this."

"That's good advice, missy," Stockton said. He felt

sure that Ward could take the big stranger, and was looking forward to seeing it. However, he didn't think Ward was going to push the matter if he didn't have to. He didn't know where Ward got his patience from.

"They left early this morning, heading north."

"North, you say?"

Haggerty nodded.

"Why would they head north?"

Haggerty shrugged.

"Damned if I know," he said. "All I can say is that's the way they were going when they rode out. Could be they changed direction afterward."

"Yeah," Ward said, "could be."

He looked at Stockton, who didn't know what he was supposed to say or do.

"Okay," Ward finally said. "Big man, you just move out of our way and we'll be leaving."

"You come ahead," Haggerty said, "I won't get in your way."

Haggerty moved a few feet to his left, keeping his eyes on both men.

Ward and Stockton moved down the stairs, both of them watching Haggerty.

"Another time," Ward said to Haggerty, "and this might have been interesting."

"Another time and place," Haggerty said, "and we'll find out."

The two men backed away until they were far from the house, then they turned and kept walking.

Once they were gone Haggerty went up the front steps to the door of the house.

"Are you all right, Doctor?" he asked.

"Those animals," Cross said, wiping blood from his

lips with the back of his hand. "I'm going for the sheriff."

"Seems to me you'd be getting the sheriff killed," Haggerty said, "and probably yourself, as well. I'd just wait until they left town, if I was you. Why don't you go back to your office and fix your lip?"

"Yes, yes," Cross said, "back to my office. I'm, uh, sorry I brought them here, Leena, but, uh, I—"

"No need to explain anything to me, Andrew," she said coldly.

"Yes, well, I better be going. . . ."

Cross went down the steps and hurried away.

"And you," Leena said to Haggerty. "How could you tell them which way Clint and the boys went?"

"I didn't," he said.

"What?"

"I lied."

"You lied?"

He nodded.

"People do that, you know."

"Well . . . that's wonderful, but . . . but what will those men do when they realize you lied?"

"They'll probably double back and pick up Clint's trail."

"But . . . you have to warn him."

"I think Clint Adams can handle those two himself," Haggerty said.

"But the boys, they'll be in danger. Orville . . ."

At the mention of Orville, Haggerty's attitude changed. He didn't know what it was about that boy that touched him, but something did. . . .

"Well, maybe you're right," he said. "Maybe I can catch up to them."

"Oh, yes, Ben," she said, touching his arm, "and hurry."

"I'll have to wait until those two leave," he said. "My horse is in the livery. I'll be on my way as soon as they're gone."

NINETEEN

''Why didn't you take him?'' Stockton asked as they walked back to the hotel.

''We don't need no trouble with the law, Stock,'' Ward said. ''Let's just check out of the hotel and be on our way.''

''We ain't had any rest yet.''

''I know—''

''We ain't eaten.''

''I know—''

''I ain't had a woman!''

''Will you stop whining?'' Ward snapped. ''You'll get your woman in the next town. I figure we're maybe six hours behind them now. We've got to keep moving.''

''And what are we supposed to do when we catch up to them,'' Stockton asked, ''now that they're with the Gunsmith?''

"We'll talk about that on the way."

"We're gonna need help, Ward."

"I thought of that already," Ward said. "Let's stop by the telegraph office before we head for the livery."

Haggerty caught sight of the two men and was surprised when they didn't go right to the livery. Instead, they veered off and went into the telegraph office.

He figured that would give him just enough time to mount up and ride out.

Once Haggerty had his horse saddled he told the liveryman to open the back door.

"Why you goin' out that way?"

"You'll find out soon enough," Haggerty said. "There's two men on the way here. They're going to ask you which way Adams and the two boys went this morning."

"I don't know which way they went."

"That's what you tell them," the big man said, "but if you mention me at all, I'll be back. Understand?"

The liveryman swallowed and said, "I understand."

"Close that back door behind me."

Haggerty walked his horse out, then mounted up and rode off.

"What if the big man was lying?" Stockton asked as they left the telegraph office. "What if they didn't go north?"

"You're the tracker," Ward said. "That's what you're gonna tell us, isn't it?"

When they reached the livery stable Stockton checked the tracks out in front.

"How much activity could there be in this town?" Ward asked. "Well?"

"That distinctive hoofprint isn't here."

"Let's go inside and see if they got new horses."

They talked to the liveryman, who saw no reason not to answer their questions. He also saw no reason to mention Haggerty at all, which suited him just fine.

"Two boys, sure. I got the horses they rode in on right here."

"You bought them?" Ward asked.

"Sort of. Traded, mostly."

"And what did you give them?"

Now the liveryman got a crafty glint in his eye, as if he smelled a chance to make some money.

"Well, lemme see, my memory ain't so good . . ."

Ward looked at Stockton, who hit the man in the belly. The air *whoosh*ed out of him, and Ward waited until he'd caught his breath.

"Remember now?"

Armed with a description of the boys' new horses, Ward and Stockton saddled their own animals and mounted up.

"What do we do?" Stockton asked.

"Let's head north a ways, just in case that big man was telling the truth."

"And then what if he ain't?"

"We'll double back and head West, see if you can pick up their trail."

"What about south?"

"I don't think they're goin' south," Ward said. "North or West seems likely, but not south."

"Why not?"

"These boys are headed somewhere, Stock. You think they want to go to Mexico?"

"Well, no, but—"

"North and then West," Ward said. "Either way we can head to California eventually."

"That where you think they're goin'?" Stockton asked.

"Two young boys like that, what other place would they know the name of?"

"Then why north?"

"If they wanted to go to San Francisco they'd have to head north eventually. Maybe Adams is takin' that route."

"And maybe not."

"Well, we're not gonna find out just sittin' here jawing at each other. Let's move!"

TWENTY

"I've never seen a horse like yours," Wilbur Wright said to Clint.

It was late in the afternoon, the same day they'd left Kellock. They had made pretty good time, and Clint decided to rest the boys, and the horses.

"There is no other horse like Duke," Clint said.

"How come you don't have to tie him, like you do the other horses?" Orville asked.

They were all sitting around, chewing on some jerky until Clint said it was time to move on again.

"He's not going anywhere," Clint said. "The other horses don't have his sense."

"How long have you owned him?" Wilbur asked.

"A long time," Clint said, "but I don't feel like I own Duke. I feel like we're partners."

"Partners? With a horse?" Orville asked.

"I don't know how it is back East these days," Clint

said, "but out here a man's got to be on good terms with his horse. I've seen too many men die because their horses threw them or ran off."

"Duke wouldn't do that?" Orville asked.

"Course he wouldn't," Wilbur said. "Clint just said he ain't like no other horse."

"Clint?"

"Yes, Orville?"

"How many men have you killed?"

"Now what made you ask that question?"

"Miss Leena, she told us about you—"

"You wasn't supposed to say nothing about that, Orville," Wilbur scolded his younger brother.

"It's all right," Clint said, before the younger boy could try to defend himself and an argument ensued. "I'll answer the question, sort of."

"What do you mean, sort of?" Orville asked.

"Well, Orville, I guess I've killed more men than most, but I can't tell you how many."

"Why not?"

"I don't keep track."

"You don't have notches on your gun?"

"No, I don't," Clint said. "That would be a terrible way to treat your gun."

"But I thought all killers kept count."

"Orville," Wilbur said. "Don't say that!"

"I'm not a killer, Orville," Clint said calmly. "Did Leena tell you that?"

"No, sir."

"What did she tell you?"

"That you're the Gunsmith, and that you have a reputation with a gun."

"Well, that much is true enough," Clint said. "I do have a reputation, but it's not something I'm proud of."

"Why not?"

"Because killing someone is nothing to be proud of. I hope you boys can go through your whole lives without ever killing someone. It's a bad feeling."

"I'll bet Ben Haggerty has killed a lot of men," Orville said.

"Maybe he has," Clint said. "I wouldn't know."

"And I'll bet he's proud of it, too," the younger Wright brother said.

"I hope he's not," Clint said.

"I'll bet Haggerty's not as good as Clint at anything," Wilbur said.

"Is too," Orville said. "He's younger and stronger."

"Is he?" Wilbur asked.

"Well, he's sure younger and bigger," Clint said.

"And strong!" Orville insisted.

"Maybe he is," Clint said. "It wouldn't surprise me."

"I'll bet he can't shoot as good as you can," Wilbur said.

"Can't say I know that for sure, Wilbur," Clint said. "I've never seen him shoot."

"Have you ever seen anybody who could shoot better than you?"

"Maybe one or two men," Clint said, "but they're dead now."

"And you ain't," Wilbur said. "That makes you better than them."

"I don't know if just being alive makes me better," Clint said. "One of them was shot in the back by a coward." Of course he was talking about his friend, Wild Bill Hickok.

"Why is that being a coward?" Orville asked. "If

somebody's faster than you, why can't you just shoot them in the back?"

"It's not fair, Orville," Clint heard himself say, when he knew all along that "fair" was not a word that entered into a lot of men's vocabulary. "A man has to have an even chance to defend himself."

"You've never shot anybody in the back?" Orville asked.

"No, I haven't."

"And he's still alive," Wilbur said.

"I'll bet Ben hasn't ever shot anyone in the back," Orville said, pushing his chin out pugnaciously.

"I'll bet he hasn't," Clint said. "I think that's enough talk for now, boys. We should get moving again."

The boys both got up, ran to their horses, untied them from the trees they were tied to, and mounted up. There was no fire to put out so Clint just walked to Duke and mounted up.

As they rode away from their cold camp, Wilbur and Orville were still debating the question of who was better, Clint or Ben Haggerty.

Clint decided to stay out of the discussion for a while.

TWENTY-ONE

It didn't take Ward and Stockton long to determine that Clint and the boys had not gone north after all.

"I knew that big fella lied," Stockton said. "You shoulda killed him."

"Look," Ward said, "we know the boys were there because their horses are there, and now we know they didn't go north. We just have to go back and pick up their trail."

"And that big fella gets away with lyin' to us?"

"We'll run across his trail again soon enough," Ward said.

"I wish I could think like you, Ward, but I can't," Stockton complained. "We shoulda killed him when we had the chance."

"Let's just turn around and go back."

"To Kellock?" Maybe Ward was going to want to

stay overnight in town, and Stockton could finally get himself a woman.

"No," Ward said, "we'll travel southwesterly and catch their trail after they left town."

"We'll catch somebody's trail," Stockton said, "but who's to say it will be theirs?"

"We'll find that out when we catch up to them," Ward said. "Besides, you don't want to catch up to them so all-fired fast anymore, do you? Not and go against the Gunsmith."

"You can't take Clint Adams with a gun?" Stockton asked Ward.

"Stock," Ward said, "there ain't a man alive can take Clint Adams with a gun . . . not alone."

"How do you know that?"

"I've seen him."

"Is he as fast as they say?"

"Faster," Ward said, "and a deadly shot. The man just doesn't miss."

Stockton scratched his chin.

"Well, maybe you're right, Ward," he said finally. "Maybe we don't want to catch up to him so all-fired fast."

"Just listen to me when I talk, Stock," Ward said, "that's all you've got to do."

"Yeah, yeah, okay."

"Besides, if there's any wild gunplay around those boys they might get shot. We don't get paid if they're both dead."

"What about if one's dead?"

"As long as one of them is alive," Ward said, "we get our money."

"I wonder what them boys know?"

"You're being curious again, Stock," Ward said. "That's a habit you're gonna have to break."

TWENTY-TWO

When they made camp that night Clint gave the job of taking care of the horses to Wilbur and Orville. He built a fire and started dinner. He made a full pot of coffee, secure in the knowledge that it would all be for him, which suited him just fine. He had a dinner of bacon and beans on the fire by the time the boys finished with the horses. They'd get better at it with each passing night, he was sure.

Clint dished out the dinner and handed them each a plate. He put a canteen nearby so they could drink water with their food.

"Can I have some coffee?" Wilbur asked.

"Coffee?"

"You don't drink coffee," Orville said.

"I can start."

"You're too young."

"I am not," Wilbur said. "I'm fifteen. I'm almost a man."

"He's got a point there, Orville," Clint said. "Sure, Wilbur, you can have some coffee."

He poured out a cup and handed it to him.

"We don't have any milk or sugar," Clint said, "but I usually drink it just like that."

"I'll drink it the way you do."

Clint watched while Wilbur took his first sip. He tried not to make a face, but he couldn't disguise the shudder that went through him.

"How is it?" Orville asked.

"It's good," Wilbur said, putting the cup down on the ground between his feet.

"Yeah, sure," Orville said. He looked at Clint and gave him a sly grin.

"You boys ready to tell me why you're going to California?" Clint asked.

The boys exchanged a glance, and Orville looked away from Wilbur, into the fire.

"Don't do that, Orville," Clint said.

"Do what?"

"Don't look into the fire."

"Why not?"

"Because when you look into the fire it blinds you. It takes away your night sight, that is. Once your eyes get used to the dark you have to be careful not to look into the flames. While your eyes are adjusting all over again, someone could sneak up on you."

"Wow," Orville said. "Like Indians?"

"Sure, Indians, and some bad white men, too," Clint said. "Also, some animals."

"Animals?" Orville said, looking around. "Like . . . what kind?"

"Bears," Clint said, "wolves, mountain lions."

"We ain't in the mountains."

"Sometimes," Clint said, "they come down from the mountains."

Orville looked around again. This time it was Wilbur's turn to slyly grin at Clint. He knew that his brother was being teased.

He hoped his brother was just being teased.

"Clint?" Wilbur said.

"Yes?"

"Do you think I should have a gun?"

"Do you know how to fire a gun, Wilbur?"

"Well . . ."

"He don't," Orville said. "Neither one of us do. And if he gets one, I have to get one, too. It's only fair."

"First of all," Clint said, "you have to stop thinking that you're entitled to everything your brother is. He's older than you are by what . . . three years?"

"Three years and a month," Wilbur said.

"There are going to be certain things that he'll be ready for and you won't," Clint went on. "There are some things you just have to wait for, Orville."

"It's not fair," Orville mumbled.

"Life isn't very fair, Orville," Clint said. "The sooner you learn that the better off you'll be."

"So then you think I should have a gun?" Wilbur said.

"No, I don't," Clint said. "You've never even held one. A gun in the hands of someone who is inexperienced is more dangerous than ever."

This seemed to mollify young Orville.

"Could you teach me how to shoot, then?"

Clint thought a moment, then said, "Yeah, I could do that."

Orville's head came up quickly, a surprised look on his face, followed by disappointment.

"When?" Wilbur said.

"We'll have to see," Clint said. "Certainly not tonight. You can't learn how to shoot in the dark."

"Tomorrow?"

"I don't know," Clint said. "That will depend on where we are. If we find a likely spot, maybe."

Wilbur happily picked up his coffee, took a big swallow, and then choked on it.

That seemed to make Orville feel better . . . but not much.

After dinner Clint showed the boys how to clean out the plates and frying pan with sand, because they had no spare water to do it with.

"Now they'll be dirty next time we use them," Orville complained.

"By that time we should come upon some water to wash them with first. This way none of the food will stick to them."

They put away the cooking and eating utensils, and then Clint decided that they would set a watch, if for no other reason than to have the boys learn something while they were in his company.

"Who wants to go first?" Clint asked.

"I'm sleepy," Orville said. "Wilbur can go first. After all, he is older."

"I'll go first," Wilbur said.

"Okay," Clint said, "then you wake up Orville in three hours."

"Okay."

"Orville, you wake me up in three hours. That way I can start breakfast before I wake you boys up."

"Okay."

"If either of you see anything or hear anything you think I should know about, wake me up right away, understand?"

Both boys nodded.

"Okay. I'm going to turn in."

"Me, too," Orville said.

"Wilbur," Clint said, "listen to Duke. He'll act up if he hears something you don't."

"All right."

Clint rolled himself up in his blanket, fairly confident that nothing would interrupt his sleep for six hours.

TWENTY-THREE

Orville was scared.

He'd never have admitted it to Clint, but he was a hair away from waking Wilbur and telling him. He had been on watch only about a half hour and for that whole time he had been hearing all kinds of noises.

He remembered what Clint said about not looking into the fire and made sure he never did. In fact, being told not to look into the fire made it suddenly very difficult. He could feel the heat from the fire and sometimes it felt as if it were teasing him. He studiously avoided the fire, and after the first half hour his neck started to hurt.

Several times he thought he saw some kind of animal, but he would look over at Clint's horse, Duke, who was standing calmly. He remembered what Clint said about Duke and realized that his imagination was running away with him.

After about an hour his neck hurt so much, and he

was so scared, that he was about to wake his brother when he heard a definite sound. It was a snapping sound, like someone had stepped on a piece of wood.

He froze and listened intently, and although he didn't hear anything more after that he noticed that Duke was restless.

He forgot about waking his brother and went right to Clint's bedroll. He shook Clint vigorously, and he came awake immediately.

"What is it?"

"I heard something," Orville said, "and so did Duke."

Clint took a good look at the boy and saw that his eyes were wide with fear. Then he looked over at Duke, who was shifting about uncomfortably.

"Okay," Clint said, rolling out of his blanket, "wake your brother and keep quiet."

Clint drew his gun and listened intently. After a few moments he almost gave up, but then he sensed more than heard something. Someone was moving around out there. He couldn't hear him, but he knew he was out there.

"Hello out there!" he called. "Show yourself."

After a moment a voice said, "Hello the camp."

"Who is it?" Clint called out.

"It's Ben Haggerty," the voice called. "Can I come into the camp?"

"Ben!" Orville said excitedly, but his older brother hushed him up.

"Can I come in?" Haggerty called.

"Come ahead," Clint said, "but do it slowly."

They all waited a few moments until Haggerty appeared from out of the darkness, stepping into the circle of light thrown off by the campfire, leading his horse.

"Haggerty," Clint said.

"I told you who it was."

"So you did," Clint said, holstering his gun.

"Hi, Ben!" Orville called out.

"Hi, Orville," Haggerty said. Clint was surprised at how happy the big man seemed to be to see the boy.

"What are you doin' here, Ben?"

"I was just riding your way, kid," Haggerty said. He looked at Clint and asked, "Mind if I share your camp?"

"You're welcome," Clint said. "There's some coffee on the fire."

"I'll take care of my horse, first."

"Can I help, Ben?"

"Aren't you supposed to be asleep?"

"Naw," Orville said, "it's my watch."

"Okay, then," Haggerty said. "Do you know how to unsaddle a horse?"

"Sure."

"Take care of him, then," Haggerty said, holding the reins out to the boy, who grabbed them eagerly.

Haggerty approached the fire, and Clint handed him a cup of coffee.

"Wilbur," Haggerty said, "why don't you go and help your brother with my horse."

Wilbur looked at Clint, who nodded.

"What's going on?" Clint asked when both Wilbur and Orville were out of earshot.

"There are two men on your trail," Haggerty said. "They rode into Kellock a few hours after you did."

"Looking for me?"

Haggerty shook his head.

"They're lookin' for the boys."

Clint frowned and asked, "Why?"

"I don't know," Haggerty said, "but they're hard cases. A couple of pros. They worked over the doctor so he told them about Leena's boardinghouse."

"Is she all right?" Clint asked.

"Yes. I stepped in and told them you went north."

"That won't fool them for long," Clint said, "but I appreciate it."

"When they do find out I lied they'll be back on your trail."

"We'll have to watch our back trail," Clint said. "What are you going to do now that you told us?"

"I thought if it was okay with you I'd ride along with you for a while."

"It's fine with me."

"There's one other thing," Haggerty said.

"What?"

"They know who you are."

"That's just great."

"Maybe it will keep them away," Haggerty suggested.

"I doubt it," Clint said. "If they're pros they'll probably just get some more help. That means we have to watch our backs and our fronts."

"Maybe they won't pick up your trail."

"That's not likely either," Clint said. "The boys came from the east, and these men must have trailed them most of that way. The question is, why?"

"How do we get the answer?" Haggerty asked. "Should we lay a trap for these men?"

"I think we have to find out what we're up against, first, Ben . . . can I call you Ben?"

"Sure," Haggerty said, waving a hand negligently. "How do you propose we find out what we're up against?"

Clint looked over to where the boys were brushing Haggerty's horse.

"I guess we'll just have to ask them."

Stockton and Ward were also camped for the night. They had ridden north just long enough to determine that Clint Adams and the boys had not gone that way, and then had headed west. They felt they were now going in the right direction, and Ward had sent some telegraph messages ahead to some people who could help. They'd keep an eye out for the boys, and they'd be available to help out with Clint Adams.

Stockton was still complaining about not having had a woman in weeks, but Ward turned a deaf ear. He was more concerned with getting their money than getting his partner a woman.

When they had their money, Stockton would be able to buy all the women he needed.

TWENTY-FOUR

When the boys were done they came back over to the fire, where Clint and Haggerty were drinking coffee.

"Am I still on watch?" Orville asked.

"We're all up now, Orville," Clint said. "Why don't you and Wilbur sit down? We have something we want to talk to you about."

The boys sat on the ground and studied the two men curiously.

"What's this about?" Wilbur asked.

"First Ben has something to tell you."

Both boys gave Haggerty their attention while he told them about the two men who had come to Kellock looking for them.

"Did they hurt Miss Leena?" Wilbur asked.

"No," Haggerty said, "she's fine."

"Why were they looking for us?" Wilbur asked.

"That's what we were hoping you could tell us, Wilbur,"

Clint said. "Why would two men be after you?"

Wilbur never looked at Orville, he just shrugged and said, "I don't know."

"I don't think that's the truth, Wilbur," Clint said, shaking his head.

"Why not?"

"You boys have been traveling a long way and you pushed your horses to the brink of death. Why is that?"

"We want to get where we're going," Wilbur said.

"It wasn't because you knew someone was after you?" Haggerty asked.

"No."

The look on Wilbur's face was like a closed and locked door. There was no way they were going to get it open without the key.

Orville, however, looked uncertain.

"Orville?" Ben asked. "Have you got something you want to tell us?"

Orville looked at Wilbur this time, who returned the look with no expression.

"Orville?"

"What do they want with us, Ben?" Orville asked.

"Well, I'm not really sure, Orville."

"Do they want to hurt us?"

"I'm not sure," Haggerty said, "but they sure looked like the kind of men who could."

Orville looked at Wilbur again.

"Don't say anything, Orville," Wilbur finally said.

"Well, well, Wilbur," Clint said, "you just made your first mistake."

"What?"

"We now know that you're lying," Clint said, "and that you do have something to hide."

Wilbur chose that moment to just press his lips tightly closed.

"My guess is these men mean to hurt you, Wilbur," Clint said, "both of you. If you want me and Ben to protect you, you're going to have to give us a good reason."

"Wilbur . . . ?" Orville asked.

"Be quiet!"

Orville gave Clint and Ben each a pleading look.

"Are you gonna leave us?" he asked.

"Why don't you and your brother go to sleep, Orville," Clint said. "Ben and I will stand watch."

"You won't leave us while we're asleep?" Orville asked.

"No," Clint said, "we wouldn't do that to you."

Orville looked somewhat relieved, but still scared.

"We are going to talk to you again in the morning, though," Clint said.

"And we're going to want some answers then," Haggerty chimed in.

"Go on," Clint said, "go to sleep."

Wilbur, looking stubborn, went to his blanket. Orville gave both Clint and Ben a last, long look, then went to his blanket and rolled himself up in it.

"What do you think?" Clint asked Haggerty. "Are we going to get any answers in the morning?"

"One way or another, Clint," Haggerty said, "we'll get an answer."

TWENTY-FIVE

Clint and Haggerty split the watch the rest of the night so the boys could sleep. Clint took the last watch and had a pot of coffee on the fire when Haggerty got up.

"What about them?" Haggerty asked.

Clint handed him a cup of coffee.

"Let's let them sleep for a while longer," Clint said, pouring himself some. "I want to talk to you."

"About what?"

"About what you're doing out here."

"I came out to warn you," Haggerty said. "I thought you'd be grateful. Instead you're questioning me."

"If you're going to ride with us, Ben, I have to be able to trust you."

"What about me trusting you?"

Clint smiled.

"I'm not asking you to trust me."

"And I'm not asking you to trust me."

"But you are asking to ride along with us," Clint said. "How do I know you're not here for some totally other reason?"

"Like what?"

"I don't—"

"Do you think I would hurt those boys?"

"I don't know you, Ben," Clint said. "The whole time I was at Leena's boardinghouse we didn't exchange more than two words."

Haggerty thought for a moment and then said, "Okay, okay, you have a point."

"So tell me what you want."

"I just want to ride along for a while and keep those boys safe," Haggerty said.

"You're really taken with Orville, aren't you?"

Haggerty looked into his coffee cup.

"Yes, I am."

"Why?"

Now Haggerty looked up at Clint.

"I was afraid you were going to ask me that."

"If you don't want to tell me—"

"He reminds me of somebody." Haggerty said it very fast, as if he wanted to get it out before he changed his mind.

"Who?" Clint asked.

"I had a son once," Haggerty said. He worried his bottom lip between his teeth. "Let's just say if my son had lived he would be about that boy's age."

"And you just want to keep him safe."

Haggerty nodded.

"Him and his brother."

"And what about me?"

"You? You can take care of yourself. I know who you are."

"And so do these hard cases. Knowing who I am, these men can't just let it go. They're going to have to go up against me to prove something to themselves."

"But you also said they won't come after you until they get some more help," Haggerty said.

"That's right. They're going to want to make sure the odds are in their favor."

"But I'm here," Haggerty said, "and they don't know that."

"And that might turn the odds in our favor," Clint said, "depending on how much help they get."

"We're gonna have to be real alert."

"Alert, yes," Clint said, "but I think we have a few days yet."

"A few days for what?"

"To find out what these boys are up to," Clint said. "I think it's time to wake them up."

TWENTY-SIX

The boys did not wake easily. Orville rubbed and rubbed at his eyes and couldn't seem to clear them. Wilbur yawned several times and shook his head. Clint wondered how much of it was an act and how much was real.

"You want some coffee, Wilbur?" Clint asked.

"Huh? Oh, yeah . . . uh, thanks."

"Hungry for breakfast, Orville?" Haggerty asked.

"Yeah!"

"Then come on."

Both boys rolled out of their blankets and sat by the fire. When they each had a plate of food in front of them—and Wilbur had his coffee—Clint and Haggerty sat on the other side of the fire and regarded them.

"Boys, I think it's time we had a real talk," Clint said.

"About what?" Wilbur asked.

"We think you know," Haggerty said.

Orville looked at Wilbur, and then at Haggerty.

"What about it, Orville?" Haggerty asked. "You want to tell us what's goin' on?"

"If Wilbur says it's okay," Orville said.

Wilbur looked at his brother.

"You think they're gonna believe us?" he asked.

"Try us," Clint said. "We just want to help you."

Wilbur looked at Clint and Haggerty, and then back at his brother.

"You wanna?" Orville asked.

Wilbur rolled his eyes and put his plate down.

"We're on our way to California to look for gold."

Clint and Haggerty exchanged a glance.

"For what?" Haggerty asked. "Are you looking to get rich?"

"No," Wilbur said, "we just want to get enough to . . ." He paused.

"To what?" Clint asked.

Wilbur took a deep breath and said, "To build a flying machine."

There was a stunned silence during which the two men simply stared at the two boys.

"See?" Wilbur said to Orville. "I told you they wouldn't believe us."

"Now, wait, wait," Clint said, holding up his hands, "wait a minute, we're willing to listen . . . aren't we?" He looked at Haggerty.

"About flying?"

"We can do it," Orville said. "We can build a flying machine."

Haggerty looked at Orville dubiously.

"It can be done," Wilbur said.

"Now, what exactly do you mean by a 'flying machine'?" Clint asked.

"A vehicle," Wilbur said, "that can fly, carrying a man in it."

"Oh, God," Haggerty said, shaking his head.

"You have to believe us, Ben!" Orville said.

"Why does he have to?" Wilbur asked his brother. "Nobody else has."

"Is that why you left home?" Clint asked. "Because nobody would believe you?"

"And because we need money to build it," Orville said.

"And you expect to get that in California."

Orville nodded.

"There's gold in the ground there."

Clint studied the eager, naive look on Orville's face and kept himself from telling the young boy that most of the gold mines in California had played out a long time ago. But what did the boy know of mines? He probably expected to find the streets in California paved with gold, much the way the Chinese had expected when they first came to this country. Instead of finding gold they found themselves laying railroad track and doing other people's laundry.

"Okay," Clint said, "let's say you get to California, and you get your gold. Then what?"

"Then we buy what we need to build our machine," Wilbur said.

"Will you let your family know where you are?"

"Sure," Wilbur said. "We'll send them a telegram. Once we're there, they can't make us come back, and it will take them a long time to get there to bring us back."

Clint didn't want to point out that their parents would have the money to travel by railroad, and would get to

California much more quickly than they would have been able to.

''And you won't tell us where you're from, or who your parents are, before you reach California?'' Haggerty asked.

Orville shook his head, and Wilbur said, ''No, we won't.''

Haggerty looked at Clint.

''Where does that leave us?''

''Back where we started, I guess.'' Clint looked at the boys and said, ''Why don't you go and saddle your horses.''

''We're still going on?'' Wilbur asked.

''Yes,'' Clint said, ''we're still going on.''

Orville looked excited, but Wilbur looked more suspicious as they got up and walked over to where the horses were.

''Do you think they're crazy?'' Haggerty asked Clint.

''No,'' Clint said.

''Then what?''

''I think they're adventurous. Weren't you when you were a boy?''

''Sure,'' Haggerty said, ''but that meant I climbed trees. I never once talked about building a flying machine.''

''Did you ever think about it?'' Clint asked, while he stomped out the fire.

''No.''

''Never thought about flying?'' Clint asked. ''What it would be like if you were a bird?''

Haggerty hesitated.

''You did, didn't you?''

''Maybe . . . maybe once or twice.''

''And you weren't crazy, were you?''

"No," Haggerty said, "but these boys really seem to think they're going to build a flying machine."

"And who's to say they won't?" Clint asked.

Haggerty stared at Clint for a few seconds and then said, "You're as crazy as they are."

"I'm not crazy," Clint said, "but why tell them they are? Let them believe what they want."

"And what are you gonna do?" Haggerty asked. "Go all the way to California with them?"

Clint thought that over for a moment, then said, "Why not?"

"It's a long way."

"I've been there before."

"So have I, but—"

"And what if they do build a flying machine?" Clint asked. "Wouldn't it be something to see?"

TWENTY-SEVEN

Ward and Stockton broke camp at first light. Stockton grumbled about doing so without even a cup of coffee, but Ward wanted to get to the next town as soon as possible. He only hoped that it had a telegraph office. He still had some more ideas about people to contact.

"Who are you sending all these telegraph messages to?" Stock asked as they started to ride.

"Just some people."

"Like who?"

Ward reeled off some last names.

"Bennett . . . Hayes . . . Watchman . . ."

"I know those boys."

"I know you do."

"They're all gonna want a cut."

"They'll get paid," Ward said. "There's no point in giving them any sort of fair cut."

"Yeah, but still, when you pay them that's gonna leave even less for us."

"I've been thinking about that, Stock."

"About what?"

"Well, we hired on to catch some kids, right?"

"Right."

"And now we're chasing some kids, and Clint Adams."

"That's right."

"Well, they can't expect us to go up against Adams for the same money."

"They can't?"

"No, they can't," Ward said. "When we get to the next town with a telegraph line I'm gonna send a message back East and see how much more money we can get."

"Do you really think you can do it?"

"Sure," Ward said. "They'll know who Adams is. They'll know his rep, and I'll tell them I need to hire more men to handle him. They'll come across with more money, you wait and see."

They rode in silence for a few moments and then Stockton asked, "How much more?"

"Probably enough so that you can buy yourself all the women you'll ever need."

They rode in silence for a little longer before Stockton spoke again.

"Ward?"

"Yeah?"

Shaking his head, Stockton said, "I don't think there's that much money in the world."

Ward looked at him and said, "Well, you'll just have to make do."

TWENTY-EIGHT

Over the next few days Clint decided not to press the Wright boys on anything. Instead, the four of them traveled together well, falling into a pattern of each doing their jobs when they camped.

Clint found himself liking Haggerty, while also feeling sorry for him. The relationship between the big man and the youngest Wright brother seemed to be deepening, and he felt that Haggerty was opening himself to more hurt by opening himself up to the boy. If Haggerty was looking to replace his own lost son he was going to be disappointed. The Wright boys already had parents, and sooner or later they would be reunited with them.

His own relationship with Wilbur was moving more slowly. Although the boy clearly preferred him over Haggerty, he still had not come to completely trust him. Until that happened the boy would never be able to open up to him.

Clint didn't really know why he'd agreed so easily to accompany the boys all the way to California. It just seemed to be the thing to do at the time. Also, he didn't quite know what to make of their talk of a flying machine. It sounded like some sort of "flight" of fancy to him, but he didn't know if such a machine was possible to make. Before he dismissed their talk, he probably should look into it. And he didn't think they should be dismissed simply because of their ages. At fifteen Wilbur was almost a man, and Orville was bright.

Clint looked over at Haggerty and wondered what was going through his mind. Aside from wanting to keep the boys safe, the big man did not seem to have any other motive for tagging along all the way to California.

From their first meeting Clint would not have thought Haggerty capable of that kind of selflessness, but obviously he was wrong. There was obviously more to Ben Haggerty than met the eye, which was something that young Orville had seen right from the beginning. Leave it to a child to see inside a man.

Clint felt badly for misjudging the man, because he knew how often he himself had been misjudged by people. Maybe, too, that was why he was willing to give the boys the benefit of the doubt. Apparently, they had reasons for wanting to get to California, just as he had his reasons for helping them.

Which brought him back to the fact that he didn't know his own reasons any better than he knew theirs.

TWENTY-NINE

Wendell Ward came out of the telegraph office in Russell, Oklahoma.

"Well?" Stockton asked.

"They been spotted."

"By who?"

"Bennett."

"Where?"

"They were in Cromwell yesterday."

Stockton snapped his fingers.

"We're a day behind them."

"I told Bennett to stay with them," Ward said, "but we've got to close the gap."

"Oh, now wait a minute—"

"We have to leave town now."

"I just need an hour."

"We have to leave, Stock."

"A half an hour," Stockton pleaded.

He saw that Ward was wavering.

"Come on, Ward," he said. "Isn't there somethin' you want to do, just for a half hour?"

"Well . . . maybe . . ." Ward said.

"Where should we meet?" Stockton asked gleefully.

"Right here," Ward said. "Right back here in half an hour."

"What are you going to do?"

"Just go and do what you're going to do and never mind."

"You're gonna contact them again, ain't you?"

The first time Ward had contacted the people who'd hired them they had argued, back and forth, over the telegraph wire. They didn't want to come up with any extra money for the Gunsmith. They maintained that Ward and Stockton were being paid "sufficiently" for the job they'd been hired to do. Ward argued that there was more to it now that the Gunsmith was involved.

Their employers were unwavering.

"What do we do now?" Stockton had asked.

"We keep going."

"And how are we gonna get help against the Gunsmith?" Stockton asked. "Pay for it out of our own pockets?"

"We'll cross that bridge when we come to it."

"You could talk to them again."

"Yeah," Ward had said, "I could."

Now he *was* thinking about contacting them again.

"Maybe I am," he said. "You go and get yourself a girl and don't worry about it."

Stockton went off, happy and anxious to find a whore. Ward wondered if he'd actually be able to find one and do what he had to do in a half hour.

Ward turned around and went back inside to renew his argument with his employer.

THIRTY

''We're being followed,'' Haggerty said.

''I know,'' Clint said. ''Since Cromwell.''

''How many do you make it?''

''Two, or three,'' Clint said. ''I've only seen two at a time, and not necessarily the same two.''

''That's what I make it,'' Haggerty said. ''I wonder what they want.''

The boys were riding up ahead, and the two men were hanging back so they could talk.

''Well, we've got two choices,'' Clint said. ''They either want the boys, or me.''

''How do we find out which?'' Haggerty asked.

''I don't think we have to do anything at the moment,'' Clint said. ''They're hanging back, so that means they're just keeping an eye on us.''

''For someone else, then.''

Clint nodded.

"Maybe those two men you tangled with back in Kellock," Clint said.

"That would make sense," Haggerty said. "They're gonna have to catch up with us. They could have sent a telegraph message ahead. They'd want more help anyway, with you involved."

"Well, right now their help is just watching," Clint said, "and as long as we know they're watching us, we can watch them."

"Hey," Orville shouted back at them, "you two are slowpokes."

Haggerty waved.

"You mind my asking?" Clint said.

"He died," Haggerty said, as if he was reading Clint's mind. "He just died."

"How old would he be now?"

"Orville's age."

They rode in silence for a while.

"I know what you're thinking," Haggerty said finally.

"I . . . didn't want to open any old wounds, but I'm . . . worried. . . ."

"That I'll get too close?"

"Yes."

Haggerty looked at Clint, and there was a haunted look in his eyes.

"I've thought about that."

"Are you getting too close?"

Haggerty looked ahead again.

"My son died because I couldn't help him, Clint," Haggerty said. "Maybe I can help Orville, and his brother. I think they're in danger from those two men."

"I do, too."

"So why don't we just keep them safe, and worry about other things later?"

"Okay."

After a few moments Haggerty said, "Maybe I'll even tell you about it . . . sometime."

Clint had always thought that a man's private pain was just that, private, but he also knew that it sometimes helped to talk to someone about it. He had the feeling Ben Haggerty had been keeping something bottled up inside for a long time. If and when he decided he wanted to talk about it, Clint would be more than willing to listen.

"Let's catch up to them before they want to know what we're talkin' about," Haggerty said.

"Right," Clint said. "For now they don't need to know that we're being followed."

Haggerty nodded. They each kicked their horse in the ribs a little and easily caught up to the two boys.

"Are you getting tired?" Orville asked them.

"Duke doesn't get tired," Wilbur said, before Clint or Haggerty could answer.

"We're not tired," Haggerty said. "We just thought we'd bring up the rear for a while."

Wilbur looked at both of them.

"We're being followed, aren't we?"

Clint and Haggerty exchanged a glance.

"How long have you known?" Clint asked.

"Since Cromwell."

"You're observant."

"I saw him, too," Orville chimed in.

Wilbur looked at Clint and said, "No, he didn't."

"Yes, I did."

Clint gave Wilbur a look that meant he understood.

"Come on, Orville," Haggerty said, "let's ride up ahead for a while."

"Okay."

Clint silently thanked Haggerty. Now he'd be able to talk freely with the older boy.

THIRTY-ONE

"Why is someone following us?" Wilbur asked.

"We don't know."

"But you could guess."

"Anybody could guess."

"Are they after you, or us?"

"Could be either one."

"Probably us, huh?"

"Are you scared?"

Wilbur hesitated, then said, "Not as long as we're with you."

"Wilbur, do you know why these men are after you?" Clint asked.

"No."

"But you could guess, couldn't you?"

"Anybody could guess."

"Good point."

They rode in silence for a while before Clint tried again.

"Okay, Wilbur," he said, "guess for me."

"Our flying machine."

"What?"

"I think they're after our flying machine."

Clint didn't know how to react to that.

"Wilbur, do you have anything . . . written down about this machine?"

"No," Wilbur said, "I have it all in my head."

"And Orville?"

"Him, too."

That meant that one boy might do as well as two—that is, if someone was actually after them for their flying machine.

"If they're after us," Wilbur asked, "why haven't they come any closer?"

"I don't think these are the same men who were looking for you," Clint said.

He explained the theory that he and Haggerty had come up with.

"So they're just gonna stay back there and watch us until the other men show up?"

"That's what I figure," Clint said. He didn't add that that was what he hoped.

"Why don't you just kill them?"

"How would you suggest I do that, Wilbur?"

The boy shrugged.

"I don't know. Just ride up to them and shoot them, I guess."

"And what do you think they'll be doing while I'm riding up to them?"

"I don't know."

"They'd be shooting at me," Clint said. "You've got to remember that most of the time when you're shooting at someone they're shooting back. You could get killed just as easily as you could kill them."

"Have you ever been shot?"

"Yes," Clint said. "Several times."

"Did it hurt?"

"It hurt a lot."

"Did you ever almost die?"

"Yes."

"Was it scary?"

"Very scary."

"I didn't think you were ever scared."

"Everybody is scared sometimes, Wilbur."

"I guess . . ."

"It's okay to be scared."

"I can't show Orville that I'm scared," he said. "I'm older. I have to be strong for him."

"That's good, Wilbur," Clint said. "I admire the way you look after your brother."

"You do?"

"Yes."

Wilbur started to turn, then stopped himself.

"I guess we shouldn't turn around and look, huh?"

"No," Clint said, "we'll just pretend like we don't know they're there."

"We're fooling them."

"That's right," Clint said, "we're fooling them."

THIRTY-TWO

When they camped that night they decided that Clint and Haggerty would split the watch for the night.

"Why can't we take our watch?" Orville asked, disappointed.

"We're being followed, Orville," Wilbur reminded him.

Orville had actually gotten used to taking his watch. With Haggerty and Clint sleeping nearby, he almost had his fear under control.

"Oh."

Secretly he wasn't as disappointed as he had sounded, so he didn't bother to argue.

When the boys were asleep Clint and Haggerty drank coffee, sitting across the fire from each other.

"I've got an idea," Haggerty said.

"What?"

"Whoever's following us has to be camped out there somewhere."

"Yeah."

"Maybe we should pay them a visit and ask them who they're working for."

The idea immediately appealed to Clint. During the course of the day he had become increasingly annoyed at being followed and doing nothing about it.

"I think we're thinking along the same lines," Clint said.

"It makes the back of my neck itch to have someone on my tail," Haggerty said.

"So, do you have some suggestions about how to do this?" Clint asked, since it was Haggerty who voiced the idea out loud.

"How are you at moving around in the dark?" the big man asked.

They woke the boys and told them what they were going to do.

"Can we come?" Orville asked excitedly.

"No, Orville," Clint said, "you have to stay behind with your brother."

"Aw, we're gonna miss all the fun—"

"This is not going to be fun," Clint said. "Somebody could end up being killed."

Orville's eyes widened.

"It's that dangerous?"

"Yes," Haggerty said.

"We'll wait here," Wilbur said. "You guys be careful."

"We will, Wilbur," Clint said. "Thanks."

"T-there's just one thing," Wilbur said, stammering only slightly, betraying his nervousness.

"What's that?"

"What do we do if you don't come back?"

Clint hesitated for a moment then asked, "What did you do before you met us?"

Clint and Haggerty decided that while the men following them certainly wouldn't camp close to them—unless they were stupid—they would probably be within walking distance—if you liked long walks.

They were half right. Apparently, the men were dumb enough to camp closer than they should have and the walk wasn't really that long at all.

There were three men sitting inside the circle thrown off by a fire.

"Know any of them?"

"Can't tell that well from here," Clint said, "but I don't think so."

"How do you want to do this?"

"Let's come in from two directions," Clint said. "You wait here and I'll move around to the other side. Give me . . . five minutes."

"Are you sure?"

"I'm sure."

"Okay," Haggerty said, "five minutes and then we go in."

"Remember what Wilbur said, Ben," Clint said.

"What?"

"Be careful."

"I'll be fine," Haggerty said, "just don't shoot me by mistake."

Clint shook his head and said, "Five minutes."

THIRTY-THREE

Clint circled the camp as quickly and silently as he could. He could hear the men talking loudly, which was foolish of them. Sounds carried well at night. Obviously, they weren't worried about being heard, or found. They had no idea that they'd been spotted.

Clint got into position in four minutes, counted to sixty, and then started moving toward the camp. . . .

Johnny Bennett was laughing when he saw the man step into the light thrown off by the campfire. The other two men—Lee Travis and Vince Strait—had their backs to the man. As Bennett stood up and started to go for his gun, though, they saw the big man behind him.

"Don't do it!" Ben Haggerty called out.

Travis and Strait started to rise, and Clint yelled, "Hold it right there!"

All three men stood stock-still, looking at each other.

''Just stand still,'' Clint said. ''I'm going to relieve you of your guns.''

''Don't get any ideas,'' Haggerty said.

Clint moved in close, slid each of their guns from their holsters, and tossed them into the dark. He patted the men down, and found a knife in one of their boots. He tossed that into the dark, also, and then backed away.

''Why don't the three of you have a seat,'' he said. ''We're going to have a talk.''

''About what?'' Bennett asked.

''Who are you guys?'' Strait asked.

''Whataya want?'' Travis demanded.

''Now, you fellas know the answers to all three of those questions,'' Haggerty said.

''We're the fellas you've been following all day,'' Clint said, ''and we got tired of it. We thought we'd stop in and ask you why.''

''Why what?'' Bennett asked.

Haggerty made a move that surprised even Clint. He brought the butt of his pistol down on the point of Bennett's shoulder. The man cried out in pain and grabbed the wounded area.

''We're not stupid,'' Haggerty said, ''so don't treat us like we are. Why are you following us?''

Bennett's eyes sought out Clint's. They were filled with pain, but they were also filled with fear.

''Whoever you're afraid of,'' Clint said, ''they're not here and we are. Think about it.''

THIRTY-FOUR

The three men pondered what Clint had said.

"Come on, Bennett," one of them finally said.

"Shut up!" Bennett snapped.

"I think it may be time to separate these boys," Haggerty said.

"I think you're right."

"I'll take this one into the dark," Haggerty said. He put his hand on the shoulder of the man who had urged Bennett to say something. "Come on, you."

"Whataya gonna do?" the man asked.

"You better keep your mouth shut, Travis."

"Come on, Travis," Haggerty said, using the man's name now that he knew it. He practically dragged the man to his feet. Travis was almost a foot shorter than Haggerty.

Haggerty pushed Travis ahead of him, and they went off into the dark.

"What's he gonna do to him?" the other man asked.

"What's your name?" Clint asked.

The man hesitated, looked at Bennett, and then said, "Strait."

"Well, Strait, I guess he's going to question him for a while," Clint said, "and if he doesn't get the answers he wants he'll probably be back for Bennett . . . or you."

Strait swallowed.

"Me?"

Clint frowned.

"I wonder if he took his knife with him?"

Miraculously, there was a scream from out of the dark.

"I guess he did."

"Hey," Strait said, "I'll tell you what you want to know—"

"Strait!"

The man gave Bennett a furious look.

"I just hired on to follow 'em," he said urgently, "not to get killed."

"They ain't gonna kill us."

"Who hired you to follow us?" Clint asked.

Bennett smiled triumphantly just before Strait said, "Bennett did."

Clint knew the answer before he asked, "And who hired Bennett?"

"I don't know," Strait said, "only he knows."

"That's right," Bennett said, "and you ain't scarin' me by takin' me into the dark."

Clint stood up and called out, "Ben, you might as well bring him back now."

Haggerty came out of the dark with Travis, who was rubbing his ear.

"How'd you get him to scream?" Clint asked.

"Screwed my gun into his ear."

"It hurt," Travis complained.

"Sit back down and shut up," Haggerty said. He looked at Clint. "What'd they tell you?"

"They work for him," he said, pointing to Bennett.

"Who's he work for?"

"They don't know," Clint said, "and we don't know."

Haggerty drew his gun and said, "Then we might as well kill him."

The big man pointed his gun at Bennett, but Clint stepped between them.

"I don't think so, Ben."

"Get out of the way," Haggerty said. "I'm not gonna be followed all the way by these three. If they won't talk they might as well die."

"Hey," Strait said, "I talked. We work for Bennett. He's the one who won't talk."

Haggerty and Clint stared at each other.

"He's right," Clint said. "Okay, Travis and Strait, get out."

"W-what?" Strait asked.

"Get up," Clint said, "and go."

"You mean we're free to go?"

"That's right."

"As long as you don't follow us anymore," Haggerty said. "If I see you on my back trail again, I'll kill you both."

Both men got to their feet and started for their horses.

"No horses!" Clint called out.

"What?"

"You heard the man," Haggerty said. "Grab your canteens and start walking."

"B-but it's miles to the next town!" Strait complained.

"The sooner you get started," Clint said, "the sooner you'll get there."

"But—"

"Go!" Haggerty said.

"What about me?" Bennett asked as the two men picked up their canteens and walked off into the dark.

"You?" Haggerty asked. "I think me and Clint will probably have to decide what to do with you. See, I want to kill you and he doesn't. We'll probably have to fight for you. Winner gets his way." Haggerty stood ramrod straight, increasing his already impressive height. "Who do you think will win?"

Bennett looked at Clint.

"I'll try my best, Bennett, but he's a big one."

"Use your gun," Bennett said. "He can't match you with a gun."

Clint looked at Haggerty, who already had his gun out.

"He's already got his gun in his hand," Clint said. "I'm not going to draw on a man who's already got his gun out . . . not to save your miserable life."

"Hey—"

"In fact," Clint said, "I don't even think I'll take a beating to try to save you." He looked at Haggerty and said, "He's all yours, Ben."

Haggerty grinned and cocked the hammer back on his gun.

"Wait, wait, wait, wait," Bennett said in rapid-fire fashion.

"Wait for what?"

"Let me think."

"No, no," Haggerty said, pointing his gun, "no time for thinking."

"Wait!" Bennett said. "Okay, I'll tell you—"

"Come on, Bennett," Clint said, "just say a name."

"Ward," Bennett said. "Wendell Ward."

Clint and Haggerty exchanged a glance.

"I don't know the name," Clint said.

"Me neither."

"Describe him," Clint said.

After Bennett did, Haggerty said, "That's the man. He had another one with him, too."

"That'd be Stockton, Hal Stockton. They work as a team."

"To do what?"

Bennett shrugged.

"Lots of things. Bounty hunting, mostly."

"Murder?"

Bennett didn't answer.

"Do they hire their guns out?" Haggerty asked loudly—so loudly that Bennett jumped.

"Yes!" he snapped. "Sometimes . . . yes."

Sure they did, Clint thought. They had to be killers or Bennett wouldn't have been afraid of them.

Clint and Haggerty exchanged another glance, but before either could say anything they heard something. It was the sound of a twig snapping beneath someone's boot.

It was then that Clint remembered that they had thrown Bennett's, Travis's, and Strait's guns out into the darkness, where Strait and Travis had just gone.

"Stupid," Clint said, turning quickly and dropping into a crouch.

He saw the silhouette of someone just at the edge of the camp, and the glint of moonlight off a gun barrel.

He didn't wait. He drew and fired twice, aware that Ben Haggerty also started firing just a split second after he did.

A couple of shots came from the dark, and Clint heard the sound of a bullet striking flesh. He looked at Haggerty, who seemed unharmed.

There was no more firing after that.

THIRTY-FIVE

When Clint and Haggerty returned to camp the boys were huddled together by the fire. When they saw the two men, Orville got up and ran to Ben, throwing his arms around his waist.

Wilbur simply stood up by the fire and remained there.

"We heard the shots," he said.

"We were worried about you," Orville said.

"We're fine, boys," Haggerty said. "We're just fine."

"What about those men who were following us?"

Clint looked at Haggerty, who shrugged.

"They, uh, won't be following us anymore," Clint said.

"Did you kill them?" Orville asked, looking up at Haggerty.

"Never mind," Haggerty said. "Let's get back to the fire. I want some coffee."

"You boys have to get some sleep," Clint said. "We need to get an early start in the morning."

Orville gave Haggerty another hug before letting go.

"I'm glad you're all right," Orville said. Then he looked at Clint and added, "You, too, Clint."

"Thanks, Orville."

They all went to the fire, and Haggerty put Orville back in his blanket.

"Clint?" Wilbur said.

"Yes?"

"Did you find out who they were?"

"They were just working for someone, Wilbur."

"Who?"

"I was hoping you could tell me that."

"I can't," he said. "Honestly. I don't know who would be after us."

"Do you know a man named Ward?"

"Ward?"

"Wendell Ward?"

Wilbur scrunched up his face the way boys do.

"I don't know anyone named Wendell Ward. Why?"

"He's the one who hired these men to follow us."

"He's the one looking for us?"

"Yes."

"To kill us?"

"I don't know."

Wilbur looked over at his brother, who was wrapped in his blanket and asleep already.

"Clint, I'm scared. I never had nobody who wanted to kill me before."

"It'll be all right," Clint said. "I won't let anyone kill you."

"Promise?"

What else could he say?

"I promise. You better get to sleep now."

Wilbur nodded and turned to go back to his bedroll.

"Wilbur?"

"Yeah, Clint?"

"Were you telling us the truth?"

"About what?"

"About your . . . flying machine?"

"What about it?"

"Is there one?" Clint asked, trying to be patient.

"Not yet," Wilbur said, "but there will be."

Clint nodded to himself as Wilbur rolled himself up in his blanket.

"Poor kid," Haggerty said, walking over to Clint.

"Huh?"

"Orville," Haggerty said. "He's really scared."

Clint looked at Haggerty.

"Scared enough to tell us where they came from?" Clint asked.

Haggerty frowned.

"Now you want to try and take them home?" he asked. "After you told them you'd help get them to California?"

"Ben," Clint said, "there are two killers on their trail."

"Who may have been hired just to find them, not to kill them."

"Do you want to take that chance?"

Haggerty shook his head.

"If only a stray bullet hadn't hit Bennett," he said,

"we might have been able to get some more out of him."

They'd left the three dead men by the fire, not wanting to take the time to bury them. Besides, maybe when Ward and his partner found the bodies they would take it as a message.

And maybe not.

"Just see what you can get out of Orville over the next few days," Clint said. "Okay?"

Haggerty nodded and said, "Okay."

"Why don't you get some sleep," Clint suggested. "I'll keep watch until daylight . . . which isn't far off."

"All right," Haggerty said, "but I don't think there's anyone left out there who can bother us tonight."

"That's okay," Clint said. "I'll stand watch. I'm not tired anyway."

"Suit yourself."

Haggerty turned in. Clint looked up at the sky and figured it would be daylight in two and a half, three hours.

He wondered how far behind them Wendell Ward and his partner were. He also wondered how many men Ward had recruited by telegraph who would be waiting someplace up ahead of them.

THIRTY-SIX

Hal Stockton was the first one to spot the bodies. Of course, they had seen the buzzards from far off, so they had a pretty good idea of what they'd find.

"Three of them," Stockton said.

"Bennett and his men."

"Maybe not."

"Yeah, it's them," Ward said. "They got too close and the Gunsmith picked them off."

They sat easily on their horses, looking down at the bodies.

"What do we do now?" Stockton asked. "Bury them?"

"First let's go down and make sure it's them," Ward said wearily, "then we'll decide what to do."

"It's them," Stockton said.

He had dismounted and examined the bodies while

Ward remained mounted. Now Stockton walked to Ward and looked up at him.

"Do you know the other two?" Ward asked.

"One, a man named Strait. I don't know the other one."

Ward nodded.

"How were they killed?"

"Shot," Stockton said. "One shot each for Bennett and Strait, two in the other man."

"The Gunsmith's got somebody else with him."

"What makes you say that?"

"He could have killed them each with one shot."

"So what do we do? Bury 'em?"

Ward shook his head.

"Leave them for the buzzards. We got to get to the next town. I need to send some more telegraph messages."

"More men."

"Three wasn't enough," Ward said. "We need to get more so they can stop Adams and the kids and hold them until we get there."

Stockton got back on his horse.

"You got somebody in mind?"

"Oh, yeah," Ward said, "I definitely got somebody in mind."

They found the cold camp next.

"This is where Adams and the kids were camped," Stockton said. "See the tracks? Four horses."

"I wonder who else is riding with them," Ward said.

"Another man. The footprints show two adults and two smaller tracks, probably the kids."

"Well, it doesn't matter who he is," Ward said, "he's as dead as Adams."

"Clint Adams ain't gonna be easy to kill, you know," Stockton said.

"Maybe not," Ward said, "but he's human, and he'll kill easy enough under the right circumstances."

"The right circumstances meaning enough men and guns?" Stockton asked.

"Stock," Ward said, "sometimes I think you're smarter than you let on."

"Ward," Stockton said, "with that many men and guns, those kids might get it."

"We'll take precautions to make sure at least one of them don't," Ward said.

"Which one?"

Ward shrugged.

"It don't much matter."

Truth of it was, Ward was getting pretty fed up with this chase. If he had his way he'd kill both the little bastards for leading two experienced bounty hunters and trackers this merry a chase.

"Mount up, Stock," Ward said. "We got some heavy ridin' to do."

THIRTY-SEVEN

Several days later they came to a town in Oklahoma called Yearwood. Clint decided that the boys needed a night's rest in a real bed. He also figured it wouldn't hurt him or Haggerty to suffer the same fate.

"What about Ward and Stockton?" Haggerty asked, out of earshot of the boys.

"I don't think it matters," Clint said. "If Ward is still using the telegraph to hire help, then trouble could be ahead of us, a hell of a lot closer than Ward and his partner."

Haggerty studied Clint for a few moments.

"What?" Clint asked.

"I don't know you well enough yet to read you, Clint," Haggerty said, "but . . . are you planning on sitting here and waiting for them?"

"It occurred to me," Clint said, "but if I did that I thought I'd let you go on ahead with the boys."

"And we might run into trouble there."

Clint nodded.

"We ought to talk about this more when we get into town," Haggerty said. "We might be able to figure something out."

When they rode into Yearwood they found it to be a small town with one hotel. Because it was small, though, the hotel had plenty of rooms, and they were able to get three, one for Clint and Haggerty each, and one for the boys.

"Do you have bath facilities?" Clint asked.

"Next door, at the barbershop," the clerk said.

"And a telegraph office?"

Proudly the clerk said, "We just got one. Down the street one block."

"Which way?"

"Make a right when you go out. It's past the barbershop."

Clint turned, and Haggerty asked, "Why are you interested in the telegraph office?"

"I got an idea. I have a friend who might be able to tell us something about Ward." He was thinking about Rick Hartman in Labyrinth. "You want to take the boys to their room?"

"Sure."

"And see about getting them a bath."

"A bath?" Orville asked, in disgust.

"We all need a bath," Haggerty said.

"You take baths?" Orville asked Haggerty.

"Every chance I get."

"Stop complaining," Wilbur said to his brother. "I'm dirty and I itch. I could use a bath."

Orville grumbled, but did not complain out loud.

"I'll drop your gear in your room," Haggerty said. Clint handed over his saddlebags.

"Get the boys settled and I'll meet you in the saloon in an hour."

"Think you'll have an answer by then?"

"Rick's usually pretty fast," Clint said. "If he knows anything, I'll have an answer."

"Okay," Haggerty said, "let's go, boys."

Clint watched Haggerty and the boys go upstairs, and then walked out the front door of the hotel. He was sure that the man in the doorway across the street thought he'd gone unnoticed. That suited him. Now he'd see if the man followed him or stayed where he was. That way he'd know who was being watched, him or the boys.

The other reason he'd wanted to stop overnight in a town was to find out for sure if word had gone on ahead of them by telegraph. He'd been sorry that all three men who were tailing them had been killed. Maybe now he'd be able to grab somebody, keep him alive, and put him to some use.

He turned right and headed for the telegraph office.

Standing across the street, Hank Phillips watched Clint Adams walk away from the hotel. His orders were to spot Adams and keep an eye on him, so he stepped out of the doorway and followed at what he felt was a safe distance. Since he was across the street he doubted that the man would spot him.

He didn't know that Clint Adams had been followed many times before and was used to seeing behind him.

THIRTY-EIGHT

Clint entered the telegraph office and sneaked a look over his shoulder. Once inside he was able to look out the window. He watched the man take up a position in a doorway across the street. He was not anywhere near as good at following someone as he thought he was.

"Can I help ya?" the clerk behind the counter asked.

"Yes," Clint said. "I want to send a telegram."

The man pushed paper and pencil Clint's way and said, "Jest write it out and I'll send 'er."

He quoted Clint the price per word, and after Clint had written the message out he gave him the total.

"That's fine," Clint said. "Send it."

"Yes, sir. Uh, you gonna wait for a reply?"

"I am."

The clerk nodded and sat down to send the message.

Clint remained at the counter, where he was sure the man across the street would be able to see him. Now that he knew he was being followed he had two options. He and Haggerty could team up and take the man off the street, or they could follow him and see where he led them. Was he the only man in town interested in them? Or were there more? Was he just a watcher, or was he a spotter who would now turn them over to someone else—someone with much more in mind than just watching?

As Clint had hoped, his reply from Rick Hartman came fairly quickly. He got to the saloon earlier than his planned meeting with Haggerty, and his tail came right along with him.

The place was filling up for the evening, but there were still plenty of tables left. He grabbed a beer from the bar and took a table in the back. He was interested to see if his tail would come inside or not.

Several men came in before Haggerty finally got there. Clint hadn't gotten a clear look at the face of the man who was following him, but he knew the man's build, and none of these men resembled him. Apparently, the man was content to stay outside.

Haggerty spotted Clint in the back, got himself a beer, and walked over to the table. Clint noticed that Haggerty's sheer size attracted a lot of attention—from both men and women. The men studied him and knew they'd never want to meet him in a dark alley. The women studied him and probably would have wanted to meet him anywhere.

Haggerty came to the table and sat down opposite Clint, who had his back to the wall.

"You smell like lilac water," Clint said, as the scent wafted across the table to him.

"The only way to get those boys to take a bath was to take one, too."

"I should take one myself," Clint said.

"The boys and I would appreciate it."

"I'll take care of it later," Clint promised.

"Did you send your telegram?"

"I did."

"And got your answer?"

"Yes," Clint said. "My friend's name is Rick Hartman. He owns a gambling house in Labyrinth, Texas, but he has a lot of contacts all over the country."

"And he's heard of Wendell Ward?"

"He's heard of Ward and Stockton," Clint said. "Apparently, when they were working alone they weren't very effective. Since they joined forces, though, they've become an effective team."

"Effective in what way?"

"Bounty hunting mostly, but they hire out to do mostly anything."

"And now they're looking for two little boys."

"I guess so."

"Well, if they're so good at what they do," Haggerty asked, "why haven't they found them yet? Why didn't they find them before the boys found us?"

"I have a theory about that."

"I can't wait."

At that point one of the saloon girls came over. She was a tall, full-breasted woman with long dark hair. She placed her hands on her ample hips and regarded Haggerty with a playful grin . . . and a hungry look.

"Can I get you boys anything?"

"Not just now, thanks," Haggerty said. "We're not finished with the beers we have."

She turned her attention to Clint, who didn't feel

slighted by her obvious preference for Haggerty. She was a big woman who probably preferred big men.

"How about you, friend?"

"I'll probably need another beer in a while," Clint said.

"Well, my name's Mimi. Anything you want," she said, and then looked at Haggerty again, "just call me."

"Thanks, Mimi," Clint said.

As the woman walked away, Clint said, "She was obviously very interested in you."

Haggerty did not even look the woman's way.

"She's a whore."

"She's a saloon girl," Clint said, "that doesn't necessarily make her a whore."

"I think you know better than that," Haggerty said.

Clint studied the man for a few seconds and realized there would be no arguing with him on this. There was a lot of Ben Haggerty's past he didn't know, and he wasn't ready to start digging now.

"Why don't you tell me your theory?" Haggerty prompted.

THIRTY-NINE

Clint explained his thinking. It was his opinion that Ward and Stockton were professionals, and the Wright boys obviously weren't.

"They're not used to hunting perfect innocents," Clint said. "The boys don't do anything these men can predict."

Haggerty nodded.

"That makes sense, but eventually luck runs out on you."

"Right," Clint said, "so that's where we come in."

"What do you suggest we do?"

"Did you see a fellow standing across the street when you came in?"

"You mean the one in the doorway who thinks nobody can see him?"

"That's the one."

"I saw him."

"He tailed me to the telegraph office, and then back to here."

"What do you want to do about it?"

"I'm not sure," Clint said. "Maybe he's alone, and just watching for us."

"Maybe he's spotting us for someone."

"I thought of that, too," Clint said.

"Maybe he's got help right in here," Haggerty said. "Look around, what do you see? Anybody paying too much attention to us?"

"That's hard to say," Clint said. "A man your size tends to attract attention, you know."

"What about before I got here?"

Clint shrugged.

"I wasn't attracting any undue attention that I could see."

"So maybe he's an advance man and his partners aren't here yet."

"Could be."

"Maybe we should find out."

"I guess so," Clint said.

"A bird in the hand . . ." Haggerty said.

"I know."

"How do you want to do it?" Haggerty asked.

"I'll leave, he'll follow me, and we'll take him somewhere quiet."

"Like where?"

Clint shrugged.

"I don't know the town. I guess I'll find an alley. He'll follow me, you follow him."

"Done."

"Finish your beer," Clint said. "We'll keep him waiting awhile, maybe wait until it starts getting dark."

"Did your friend fill you in on Ward and Stockton any further?"

Clint nodded.

"Ward's the gun hand," Clint said. "He's got a rep for being fast and accurate."

"And Stockton?"

"Apparently he's the tracker."

"He must be getting pretty frustrated by now," Haggerty said.

"They both probably are."

"Maybe they'll make a mistake."

"That'd be fine with me," Clint said. "Are the boys okay?"

"They're in their room," Haggerty said. "I told them to make sure they stay there."

"But they're boys."

"Meaning they might not?"

"Meaning they probably won't—unless they're scared enough."

"I think they're pretty scared."

"Did you get a chance to talk to Orville?"

"About his parents?"

Clint nodded.

"It's no good," Haggerty said. "He won't talk if Wilbur doesn't want him to."

"They're very close."

"That's the way brothers should be."

Haggerty's tone of voice led Clint to believe he was speaking from personal experience, but he decided not to ask.

"I think they'll stay put," Haggerty said.

"Good. I don't want to have to worry about them while we're taking care of our friend across the street."

Suddenly, their eyes met.

''You don't think—'' Haggerty started.

''I don't know,'' Clint said. ''I guess one of us should stay at the hotel with them, though, just to be on the safe side.''

''Then let's get this thing done,'' Haggerty said, standing.

''Right.''

They started for the door and stopped just before reaching it.

''I'll go out first,'' Clint said. ''Just give me a few seconds and then follow. You can see him from the window.''

''I'll be right behind you,'' Haggerty said, ''don't worry.''

''I'm not worried,'' Clint said.

He thought he knew Haggerty well enough at this point to know that he'd watch his back.

FORTY

Clint left the saloon and started toward the hotel. He remembered that there was an alley right next to it, and figured that would make a likely enough spot for them to question their man. Also, they'd be close to the boys.

Clint didn't bother to look behind him. He decided to trust Haggerty to have the man in his sights. Even so, the middle of his back started to itch. As far as Clint was concerned the lowest creature on God's earth was a back-shooter, like the coward who shot his friend, Wild Bill Hickok. He just hoped they weren't dealing with such a coward here.

The hotel came into view, and the alley was just before it. He wondered if this man would be dumb enough to follow him into an alley that, as dusk fell, was sure to be fairly dark.

There was only one way to find out.

• • •

Haggerty watched out the window as the man across the street vacated his doorway to follow Clint. The big man stepped out of the saloon then and started in the same direction.

The man was staying across the street, thinking that would keep him from being spotted, not knowing that he had already been spotted long ago. Actually, staying across the street would keep him from spotting Haggerty on his trail. Also, the man had no reason to think that *he* was being followed by anyone. That made it easy for a man Haggerty's size to follow him unnoticed.

Haggerty could hardly see Clint, who was about a block ahead of him. Dusk made the distance seem even further. For this reason he didn't know when Clint had turned into the alley, but was able to judge that he must have done so when the man crossed the street. Haggerty quickened his step and saw the man pause at the mouth of the alley before entering.

They had him.

Clint moved to the back of the alley where he found some crates he could hide behind. He listened intently, because sound was the only thing that would tell him if the man was following him. He thought he heard the sound of a booted foot scraping the ground, and then suddenly he could hear the sound of a man breathing through his mouth. He wondered how far behind Haggerty was—and then his question was answered as the man was suddenly pushed from behind. Clint, whose eyes were by now adjusted to the dimness of the alley, saw the man go sprawling into the dirt. He moved quickly, relieving the man of his gun before he knew what was happening.

"Nice work," Clint said to Haggerty.

"Don't thank me," Haggerty said, "thank him. He's the one who was dumb enough to follow you into this alley."

"Hey, w-what's goin' on?" the man on the ground demanded.

"Just sit tight for a minute, friend," Clint said. "We're going to be asking you some questions."

"About what? Who are you guys?"

"You know who I am," Clint said. "At least, you should, since you've been following me all day."

"Wha—followin' y—you're crazy."

"I don't think so," Clint said. "You been on my tail for hours, and we know why."

The man looked surprised.

"You do?"

"Yes, we do."

He frowned.

"How?"

"Never mind how," Clint said. "Just tell us what you're supposed to be doing for Wendell Ward."

"Wendell . . . Ward?"

The look of puzzlement on the man's face was too genuine to doubt. He wasn't smart enough to lie that well. This was another case of finding someone who had been hired by someone who had been hired by Wendell Ward.

"Ward is smart," Clint said.

"How so?" Haggerty asked.

"He hires one man, and that man hires the rest."

"You believe him?" Haggerty asked, indicating the man on the ground.

"Yeah, I do," Clint said. "He doesn't know who Ward is."

''See? I told you I didn't,'' the man said. He started to get up, but Haggerty stopped him.

''Nobody said you could get up!''

''Hey,'' the man said, ''he said I didn't know—''

''You don't know who hired Ward,'' Clint said, ''but you know who hired you. That's our next question.''

''H-hey,'' the man said again, ''I'll call the sheriff.''

''I'll cut your throat before you get a word out,'' Haggerty said.

That scared the man, even though he didn't see a knife on Haggerty.

''Why don't you just let me go?'' he whined.

''We will,'' Clint said, ''as soon as you tell us who hired you.''

''And where he is,'' Haggerty added.

''And what his plan is,'' Clint said.

''Start talking,'' Haggerty said.

The man looked up at them, seemingly close to tears, but eventually he did start talking.

FORTY-ONE

The man's name was Phillips. He'd been hired by a man named Jason to spot Clint, keep him in sight, and then send word that he'd arrived. When Jason and his men showed up, he was to point Clint out.

"Jason," Haggerty said. "Is that a first name or last name?"

"Only name I know," Phillips said. "Honest."

"Have you sent word of our arrival?" Clint asked.

Phillips nodded.

"How?"

"I paid a kid two bits to deliver the message."

"What was the message?"

"That you were in town, that you'd put up your horses at the livery and took hotel rooms."

Clint looked at Haggerty.

"He'll be certain that we're staying at least the night."

Haggerty nodded his agreement.

"Probably won't show up until morning."

Clint looked at Phillips.

"You got any idea about that?"

"I don't know what he'll do," Phillips said. "Honest."

"Where's he coming from?"

"A shack about ten miles outside of town."

"Would he have the message yet?"

"Yeah, sure."

"Do you think he'd be here by now?"

"I-if he was comin' tonight, yeah."

Clint and Haggerty exchanged a glance. They were both thinking the same thing. If they took Phillips off the street, that might tip off Jason that they knew he was coming. If they left him on the street, then he might tip off Jason, himself.

"What do we do with him?" Haggerty asked.

"Y-you said you was gonna let me go."

"If we do that," Clint said, "you'll go right to Jason."

"I won't," Phillips said. "I swear."

"If not, then you'll tip him off when he gets to town."

"I won't, I swear."

"We can't trust him," Haggerty said. "We'll have to kill him."

"Hey—Jesus—h-hey, no," Phillips blubbered. "Look, I-I'll tell Jason whatever you want me to tell him. I swear to God!"

Clint looked at Haggerty.

"What do you think?"

Haggerty looked down at Phillips, his face devoid of any emotion.

"I don't think he's scared enough to trust," the big man said.

"You can trust me!" Phillips wailed. "I swear. I'll tell Jason anything you want."

"Have you been paid?" Clint asked.

"Ha-half," Phillips said, barely able to get his words out. "H-he paid me half."

"When do you get the other half?"

"When I point you out."

"Do you want that money?"

"Hey—jeez—no, not if you don't want—"

"Calm down," Clint said. "Do you want that money, yes or no?"

"Y-yes."

"And do you want to live?"

"Yes!"

"Then here's all you have to do," Clint said. "Tomorrow, when Jason arrives, point me out."

"What?" Phillips asked.

"What?" Haggerty echoed.

"Trust me," Clint said to Haggerty, then addressed himself to Phillips again. "All you have to do is point me out. You can collect the other half of your money, and stay alive to spend it. Understand?"

"Uh, n-no—I mean, y-yes."

"How can he understand it when I don't?" Haggerty asked.

"I'll explain later," Clint said. "Right now we have to convince him to do just what we say and no more."

"Let me," Haggerty said.

He produced a knife. The handle looked like that of a bowie knife, but the blade was smaller. Clint thought it might be something Haggerty had come up with himself. Easily concealed, but the big handle made it easy to handle for a man with hands his size.

He holstered his gun, knelt by Phillips, and put his knife to his throat.

"If we let you go, you'll do what you're told, right?" he asked.

"R-right." Phillips's eyes were at first wide, and then he closed them tightly while Haggerty applied pressure to his throat with the blade.

"If you run out," Haggerty said, "I'll find you and kill you. Do you believe me?"

The man started to nod, but that made the blade bite deeper, so he said, "Yes," in a squeaky voice.

"If you meet with Jason tomorrow and tell him anything other than what you've been told, one of us will kill you. Understand?"

"Y-yes."

"This is Clint Adams," Haggerty said. "You know that, right?"

"Yes."

"Jason and his men don't have a prayer against the Gunsmith," Haggerty said. "Tomorrow afternoon we'll still be alive, and if you've done anything other than what we've told you, we will kill you. Do you understand?"

"Oh, God . . . y-yes."

"Tell me something, Phillips," Clint said.

"Open your eyes and look at him when he talks to you," Haggerty ordered.

The man opened his eyes and looked at Clint.

"Why were you chosen to point me out?"

"I-I seen you once."

"Where?"

"In Denver. I was there once and I—I seen you."

"How long ago?"

"Two, maybe three years."

Clint had been to Denver both two years ago, and three, so it made sense.

Haggerty asked Clint, "Do you think he's scared enough yet?"

The acrid smell of urine filled the alley as the man's bladder let go from sheer fear.

"I think he's scared enough," Clint said.

FORTY-TWO

After they released Phillips, Haggerty expressed some doubt about their decision.

"How do we know anything he said was true?" he asked, as they entered the hotel lobby.

"I think the fact that he wet himself might be a hint that he was scared enough, Ben."

"Yeah," Haggerty said, "but that's a humiliating thing to have happen to you, Clint. What if he wants revenge? What if he wakes up tomorrow more mad than afraid?"

Clint rubbed his chin.

"You might have a point," he said. "Maybe I should have a talk with the local law."

"You want to bring the sheriff in on this?"

"Why not?"

"He might want to hold on to the boys, seeing as how they're runaways."

"I'll just tell him that we're taking them home," Clint said, "to California."

"I just don't know about bringing the law into it," Haggerty said.

"Relax," Clint said, "if you don't want me to mention you, I won't."

"I'm not on the run or anything," Haggerty said quickly—maybe too quickly.

"I didn't say you were. I'm just saying I won't tell the sheriff any more than he has to know. Hell, when I tell him my name he's just going to figure it's somebody else trying to make a name for himself."

"I guess so."

"You go up and stay with the boys," Clint said, "and I'll see you later."

"It's probably just somebody out to make a name for himself," the sheriff said.

Clint had gone to the sheriff's office and found it locked up. He had to track the man down and, ironically, had found him in the saloon where they had been a short while ago.

He introduced himself, and the sheriff invited him to have a beer. They found a table occupied by a single man, who gave it up as a courtesy to the law.

"You don't see that very often," Clint said.

"It's a pretty law-abidin' town," Sheriff Ray Allison said. When he'd introduced himself he had added that he was "no relation" to Clay Allison, the gunman.

"That's why what you say concerns me," the man added.

"Well, the man was pretty definite," Clint said.

"Did he tell you how many men?"

"Not the exact number," Clint said, "but past experience tells me to expect at least a half a dozen men."

The man nodded and worried his mustache with his right hand while holding on to his beer mug with the left. He was dark-haired and appeared to be in his mid-thirties.

"I expect I'll have to be up early tomorrow and be on the lookout."

"Actually," Clint said, "I was just letting you know what was going on, Sheriff. I didn't expect you to take a hand."

"Then why tell me?"

"Well, first I thought you might know the man involved and be able to tell me something about him."

"Jason, did you say?"

"That's right."

The man thought a few moments, then shook his head.

"No, the name doesn't mean anything to me."

"Well, the other thing was I just wanted to let you know I was in town. I usually check in with the local law. You know, a lot of times trouble follows me, even when I'm not looking for it."

"I imagine that's true, given your reputation. I appreciate you findin' me and lettin' me know, but if there's gonna be a shoot-out on the streets, I'm not gonna just stand by and watch."

"Have you got deputies?"

"One or two, but they're not regular."

"It's doubtful that they'd take part, then."

Allison laughed.

"Not for what they get paid."

"Well," Clint said, "I guess I've done what I can."

"What about the man who brought you this news?" Allison asked. "What's his name?"

Clint hesitated, then said, "Phillips. He said his name was Phillips."

"Hank Phillips?"

"He didn't give his first name."

"It must be Hank."

"What do you know about him?"

"He hires out to do odd jobs," Allison said. "He's not a brave man, which is probably why he talked to you. Did you, uh, scare him?"

"Uh, some. My traveling companion is a big man."

"What's his name? You didn't say."

Clint realized he'd made a mistake. He'd promised Haggerty he wouldn't tell the sheriff more than he had to, and he'd just blurted out that he was riding with another man. Silently, he hoped that Haggerty had been telling the truth when he said he wasn't on the run from the law.

"Ben Haggerty."

Allison thought a moment, then shook his head.

"Should I know him?"

"I can't think of a reason why you should."

"Well, if Phillips spilled his guts about somethin', I'd say he was tellin' you the truth. He'd be too scared not to."

That, at least, was something Clint wanted to hear. He lifted his mug and drained his beer.

"Thanks for talking with me, Sheriff."

"I'll be around tomorrow, Mr. Adams. If somethin' happens, you can depend on me to be there."

Clint nodded and said, "I appreciate that, Sheriff. I hope it doesn't happen."

"So do I," Allison said. "Yearwood is usually a quiet town."

"Well, I'll be sorry if I'm the reason it gets noisy," Clint said.

"It won't be your fault, Mr. Adams," Allison said, "but the fault of the men who think they have the right to gun you down just because you've got a rep."

"That's real understanding of you, Sheriff. Other lawmen might have ordered me out of town tonight to avoid this."

Allison smiled and said, "Don't think the thought hasn't occurred to me."

FORTY-THREE

On the way back to the hotel Clint was especially alert, in case everyone was wrong about Hank Phillips, and Jason and his men were already in town. The walk to the hotel was uneventful, though. As he entered the lobby, however, he saw someone familiar, and was a bit surprised.

"Hello," she said.

It was Mimi, from the saloon. She was still wearing her saloon dress, the bodice cut low enough to show what seemed like acres of creamy flesh, even with a shawl over her shoulders.

"Hello," he said. "Are you, uh, looking for someone?"

She assumed a shy look, and he realized that she was very pretty beneath the face paint she was wearing.

"Well, uh, I was hoping to, um, catch you and your friend."

"You're interested in him, aren't you?"

"Well," she said again, "a woman my size doesn't usually run into a man his size."

Clint realized that she was a couple of inches taller than he was. A man his size, he thought, didn't often run into a woman her size. He found himself intrigued by the possibilities here.

"I suppose not."

"Do you, uh, know if he would be interested in some company?" she asked.

"I'm afraid not," Clint said. "He's, uh, well—"

"Doesn't like saloon girls, huh?" she asked.

"I'm sorry—"

"That's all right," she said, holding up one hand. The move lifted her breasts interestingly. "I got that impression anyway."

He didn't know what to say.

She smiled suddenly and said, "I do get the impression that you'd be interested, though."

"You're a lovely woman," he said, "I think a man would be a fool not to be interested. However, I don't usually, uh, pay—"

"As a matter of fact," she said. "I happen to be in the mood for some company tonight. It wouldn't cost you anything more than some, um, time and effort?"

Clint hadn't been with a woman since Leena Gill, and that felt like a long time.

"Why don't you come upstairs," he said, "and we can discuss it?"

He took Mimi to his room and left her there while he checked on Haggerty and the boys. He found the three of them in the same room, the one they had gotten for the boys. Haggerty answered his soft knock.

"How are they?" he asked.

"Asleep." The big man stepped out of the room into the hall, closing the door softly behind him. "How'd it go with the sheriff?"

Clint related his conversation with the sheriff, making it short and simple.

"Then we'll assume that Phillips will do as he was told?" Haggerty said.

"I think we should."

"What about tonight?" Haggerty asked. "Should we set watches? I can take the first and wake you in, say, four hours."

"That sounds good," Clint said. He didn't know how to introduce Mimi into the conversation, so he decided to say nothing.

"All right," Haggerty said. "I think I'll just stay in here with the boys."

"Fine. I'll see you in four hours."

Haggerty went back into the boys' room, and Clint went down the hall to his. Haggerty's own room was between his and that of the boys, so he doubted that they'd be able to hear any noise that he and Mimi made.

He entered his room, surprised at the amount of anticipation he was feeling—and guilt. But if Haggerty was on watch, what did it matter what he was doing in the privacy of his room?

As he entered he saw that she had turned the gas low on the lamp so that the room was lit just enough to see—and see her he could. She was reclining on the bed, naked, one knee lifted. Her breasts were very large and firm, and the bush between her legs seemed a huge tangle of dark hair. She was easily the tallest, and possibly the largest, woman he'd even been with.

"Come to bed, Clint," she said, reaching out to him. "I need taking care of."

He moved to the bed, discarding his clothes as he went. By the time he was standing beside the bed his penis was erect, almost painfully so.

"Mmm," she said, taking him in both of her hands, "maybe I'll take care of you first."

She drew him onto the bed, on his back, and slid down so that she was between his legs. She stared up at him while she stroked him with her hand, and he found that she had the most . . . lascivious eyes he'd ever seen. Even when she took him slowly into her mouth she never took her eyes off of his.

At one point during the next two hours he found his penis nestled between her big breasts, something he hadn't done with a woman before. He was straddling her, and she pressed her big breasts together so that there was plenty of friction as he moved his penis back and forth. Every time the tip of him popped out near her chin, she would reach for it with her tongue. He found the position extremely erotic and exciting, especially when he ejaculated and she still would not release him. His ejaculate filled the hollow in her throat and a drop glistened on her chin until she licked it off.

He realized suddenly that he was getting for nothing what a lot of men in this town had to pay for, making him an extremely lucky man. . . .

Later he knelt behind her, spread the cheeks of her majestic butt, and slid into her to the hilt. She gasped as he began to move inside of her. She was tireless, and they had tried every position manageable. He was impressed with his own ability to keep up with her, and wondered how badly he'd have to pay for it later.

Jesus, he thought, Haggerty would be calling him for his watch in a little while, and he hadn't gotten any sleep.

And it didn't look like he would be, any time soon.

FORTY-FOUR

As it turned out he managed to get an hour's sleep before Haggerty knocked on his door. He answered the door and simply nodded at the big man, wishing him good night. Haggerty still didn't know about Mimi, and the knock on the door had not awakened her.

Clint got dressed and went to the window to look outside. Now that he'd spent a few hours with the woman, he realized how irresponsible it had been to do so. They were all in danger, and he had added her to the mix.

He sat on the bed and awakened her as gently as he could.

"Again?" she asked, stretching her marvelous body. "Already?"

"No," he said, "although I wish that was why I was waking you. I think you should leave."

She looked disappointed.

"Why?"

"There's a possibility that there might be some trouble, and I don't want you to be here if it happens."

"What kind of trouble?"

He didn't want to tell her the whole story.

"The kind you don't want any part of, Mimi. Come on, be a good girl. Get dressed and I'll walk you downstairs."

She complied reluctantly, and he found himself getting aroused again just watching her dress.

"You're cute," she said.

"How so?"

She smiled.

"You're watching me like a hungry cat watches a mouse."

Now he smiled.

"You're no mouse."

"Well, you're like a cat," she said, and added, "a tiger. Will you be in town long enough for us to do this again?"

"Oh, God," he said sincerely, "I sure hope so."

They walked to the door, and he opened it quietly and took a look outside.

"Do we have to be this careful?" she asked in a low voice.

"You can never be too careful," he said. He didn't tell her that aside from the trouble he didn't want Haggerty to find out about her.

They walked quietly down the hall and down the stairs to the lobby, where they drew a knowing look from the desk clerk. They ignored him and walked to the door.

"Will you be all right walking home?" he asked.

"It's a quiet town," she said, "I walk home alone all the time."

"Well, be careful."

She put her hand on his chest and said, "Thanks for keeping me company."

"The pleasure was mine," he said.

"No," she said, "the pleasure was both of ours."

She kissed him sweetly and then went out the door. He watched her as she walked down the street, then he turned to go back into the lobby. He stopped short when he thought he saw something. He backed into the lobby, then moved to one of the front windows to peer out.

The moon was not full, but it was bright enough to throw shadows, and that was what he thought he saw. He watched for the next five minutes until he saw it again. Someone in the shadows, crossing into the light just long enough to throw a shadow.

"You son of a bitch!" he said, meaning Hank Phillips. Apparently the humiliation had been enough to overcome the fear, and he had given them up early. The shadows he was seeing now were men moving into position.

He turned and hurried to the stairs. Running up, he hoped that Hank Phillips would be among the men outside, so they wouldn't have to go looking for him later.

FORTY-FIVE

Clint pounded on both doors, intent on waking Haggerty and the boys at the same time. Sure enough, as Haggerty opened his door Wilbur also opened the door to the next room.

"What's going on?" the boy asked.

"Clint?"

"They're going to make their try before morning, Ben," Clint said. "They're outside. We've got to get the boys to a safe place."

"I'll be right there."

"Wilbur," Clint said, "get dressed and get your brother dressed."

"Yes, sir."

"And, Wilbur!"

"Yes, sir?"

"When this is over we're going to have no more nonsense. You're going to tell me everything. Do you understand?"

Wilbur hesitated, then said, "Yes, sir."

Haggerty returned to the door dressed.

"How do you want to play this?" he asked.

"I'm tired of waiting," Clint said. "I say we go outside after them."

"All right," Haggerty said. "Let's do it."

They got the key to a vacant room from the desk clerk and put the boys inside. They planted them in a corner of the room with the mattress from the bed wrapped around them as protection against errant shots.

"Don't move from this room until Ben or I come to get you. Understand?"

"Yessir," both boys said.

Clint met Haggerty out in the hall.

"I'll go out the back," Clint said.

"How will I know when to come out the front?" Haggerty asked.

"You'll know."

Outside a man named Roy Jason and five others were still getting themselves into position to launch an assault on the hotel. Little did they know that an assault was about to be launched on them.

FORTY-SIX

Clint went out the back and immediately lucked out. He walked smack-dab into a man who was getting into position behind the hotel. The man was stunned, and Clint moved first, drawing his gun and catching the man flat-footed.

"I'll brook no shit from you," Clint said. "Answer my questions or die."

"A-are you the Gunsmith?"

"I'm him."

The man raised his hands as high as he could and said, "Ask away."

Clint left the man unconscious behind the hotel when he got the information he was looking for. Five men in front of the hotel, led by a man named Roy Jason who, this man said, was a "partner" of Wendell Ward. And lastly, Hank Phillips *was* with the other five.

Clint had everything he wanted in a nice neat little bundle.

He used the alley next to the hotel to get to the main street. Jason, the man had said, had taken up position inside the closed general store across the street. How he got in didn't matter, just that he was inside.

Clint took a breath and ran across the street. If anyone heard him they'd probably think he was one of them, getting into position.

The only man who knew who it was, was Haggerty, who was watching from the main hotel window. He saw Clint run across, and drew his gun.

Jason looked at his watch. He'd given his men twenty minutes to get into position, and only that long so Art Skully could get into the hotel through the back door.

One minute left.

Haggerty could see Clint's silhouette as he made his way over to the general store. Suddenly, Haggerty saw a shadow from the corner of his eye. There was a man in front of the hotel, probably an impatient man.

He moved to the door, holstered his gun, and waited.

Clint got to the point where he could see the window to the general store. Just inside he saw a man looking at his watch.

This had to be Jason, and of all these men, this was the one he wanted alive.

"Skully?" Haggerty heard a voice call.

Obviously there was supposed to be a man inside the lobby by now.

"Skully?" More anxious.

"Yuh."

"Jesus, about time," the man said. "Everything clear?"

"Yuh."

"I'm comin' in."

The man poked his head in, and Haggerty grabbed it in both hands and twisted until he heard the neck crack. He dropped the dead man to the floor. He was pleased to see that it was Hank Phillips. Apparently, the man had acquired a bit of a backbone too late in life for it to do him any good.

Next, he thought.

FORTY-SEVEN

Haggerty made the assumption that Clint had killed at least one man, the one who was supposed to be in the lobby—Skully. With the one he'd just taken care of that made two dead or simply accounted for. Clint probably had a bead on a third in the general store.

Figure at least three left, maybe more.

He drew his gun and decided not to wait anymore. He stepped outside.

Clint heard the shot and looked across the street. Haggerty had grown impatient and stepped out too soon. As big as he was, it was probably obvious that he was not one of the attackers. Someone had fired, and Haggerty had been hit . . . but he wasn't down.

• • •

Haggerty felt the burn as the bullet went into his side, but he kept his concentration and fired at the muzzle flash. He fired twice and heard a man cry out.

Jason grew immediately angry. Someone had fired prematurely and that meant that things were not going to go according to plan. If the plan had broken down already, he was not prepared to continue with it. Not against someone like the Gunsmith.

It was time to pull out.

He opened the front door of the store, which he had forced, stepped out, and came face-to-face with Clint Adams.

"Just stand fast, Jason, and drop your gun."

"You're Adams."

"That's right."

"Take it easy," Jason said. "Here's my gun." He dropped it to the ground.

"Call out to your men, tell them it's all over. They're free to go."

"This is Jason!" the man called. "Pull out! It's all over."

Only two men were remaining, and they obeyed immediately. Clint heard the sound of horses riding away.

"Sounds like two left. You started with six."

"You killed three?" Jason asked.

"Two, I think. I just took one out of the play."

Haggerty came across the street, holding his side.

"You hit?" Clint asked.

"I'll live."

"We'll get you to a doctor after we finish with Jason."

"What do you want?" Jason asked.

"Information."

"You won't get it."

"Then you'll die," Haggerty said. His face was pale and his side was soaked with blood. Jason believed him.

"All right," he said, "I'll tell you what you want to know."

FORTY-EIGHT

The next morning Jason was in the sheriff's jail. Haggerty had been bandaged—the bullet had gone through cleanly—and he, Clint, and the boys were talking over breakfast.

''Do you boys know a man named Slaton?'' Clint asked.

Wilbur's eyes widened.

''Mr. Slaton is an acquaintance of our father,'' he said.

''Not a friend?''

''No,'' Wilbur said, ''not a friend.''

''What else do you know about this Slaton?'' Haggerty asked.

Wilbur hesitated.

''Wilbur, you'll tell us everything now,'' Clint said. ''It's time.''

"Mr. Slaton," Wilbur said, "he has an idea for . . . for a flying machine."

"What?" Haggerty asked. "A grown man talking such nonsense?"

"It's not nonsense," Wilbur said. "Our idea will work."

"Will Mr. Slaton's?" Clint asked.

"No."

"Does he know that?"

"Yes."

"And does he know that yours will work?"

"I think so."

"That's it, then," Clint said.

"What is?" Wilbur asked.

"Slaton hired Ward and Stockton to find you boys once you left home."

"North Carolina," Wilbur said.

Finally, Clint thought.

"Mr. Slaton wanted to kill us?" Orville asked.

"I don't think so, Orville," Clint said, "but he hired two men who knew how to kill. I believe at least one of you would have been taken back for Mr. Slaton to question about your ideas."

"You can't be serious," Haggerty said. "All of this over a flying machine?"

"It's got to be," Clint said. "What else could it be?"

"But . . . a flying machine?"

"We can make it work," Wilbur said.

"In California," Orville said.

"Don't you boys miss your folks?" Clint asked.

"Well . . ." Wilbur said.

"Yes," Orville said.

"If I could get somebody to invest some money in

your flying machine,'' Clint said, ''would you let us take you home?''

The boys exchanged a glance.

''After all, that's what you were looking for. Money. Right?''

''Right,'' Wilbur said.

''Who are you going to get to invest,'' Haggerty asked, ''in a flying machine?''

''I know some people with money,'' Clint said, ''and imagination.'' He looked at the Wright brothers. ''What do you say?''

''Okay,'' Wilbur said, ''we'll go home.''

''Good.''

''What about Ward and Stockton?'' Haggerty asked.

''We'll telegraph the boys' father, he'll have the law visit Mr. Slaton. I think we can get Ward and Stockton called off.''

''And if we can't?'' Haggerty asked.

''Then we'll deal with them like we did with Jason and his men,'' Clint said. ''Only this time we'll do it head-on.''

Ward came out of the telegraph office in Smithville, Oklahoma.

''What is it?'' Stockton asked.

''From one of the men who was with Jason,'' Ward said.

''What happened?''

''Two of them are dead, and Jason's in jail.''

''Did Jason talk?'' Stockton asked.

Ward looked at him.

''He did.''

''I'll kill him.''

"There's no percentage in it," Ward said. "I think we're done."

"What?"

"Do you really want to go up against the Gunsmith?" Ward asked. " 'Cause I don't."

"You don't?"

"No."

"Well . . . neither do I."

"That's it, then."

"What about the first half of the money we took?" Stockton asked.

"Let them find us and get it back," Ward said. "Come on, we'll keep heading west. I hear California's paved with gold."

"And full of good-looking women," Stockton said.

"Yeah," Ward said. "Maybe we can find a new line of work there, too. I think our luck has about run out with this one, don't you?"

Watch for

HOMESTEAD LAW

184th novel in the exciting GUNSMITH series
from Jove

Coming in April!